NEW
TOWN

Other Novels by Harry Blamires

The Devil's Hunting Grounds
Cold War in Hell
Highway to Heaven

NEW TOWN

A FABLE . . .
UNLESS YOU BELIEVE

HARRY BLAMIRES

Revell
Grand Rapids, Michigan

© 2005 by Harry Blamires

Published by Fleming H. Revell
a division of Baker Publishing Group
P.O. Box 6287, Grand Rapids, MI 49516-6287

Printed in the United States of America

Library of Congress Cataloging-in-Publication Data
Blamires, Harry.
    New town : a fable— unless you believe / Harry Blamires.
        p. cm.
    Includes bibliographical references.
    ISBN 0-8007-5997-4 (pbk.)
    1. Heaven—Fiction. 2. Future life—Fiction. I. Title.
PS3503.L39N49 2005
813′.54—dc22   2005014193

To Nancy
with love

CONTENTS

How Bernard Dayman fell asleep and came in his dream to Old Hertham, and how an old friend received him

When Bernard fell asleep, his breathing became very gentle. At first the nurse thought he had died. Bernard thought so too, because suddenly all the pain left him. The tight grip on his throat was relaxed. No longer did he seem to be nailed to a board through his neck. The stinging and throbbing in his arms and legs melted away. The amateur carpenters gave up trying to sandpaper the flesh from his bones. Instead, he seemed to float upward through waves of healing air. It was as though he had been caught in the suction stream of a cosmic vacuum cleaner. At first he was whirled gently round by the current, but gradually he became steadily upright. Then his legs started to walk of their own accord. He found himself striding freely down an urban street in morning sunshine.

It was not a street Bernard had ever walked down before, and yet there was something vaguely familiar about it. The place had the faintly rural atmosphere of a county market town, a mixture of periods in the architecture—Elizabethan, eighteenth century, Victorian, and modern. Bernard noticed an estate agent's office. It advertised itself as Godfrey and Son. The shop had a renovated front, pseudo-Elizabethan in style and freshly painted in black and white. Bernard looked in the window. There were show boards with white cards attached in neat rows. The display suggested an active market in property. Bernard stopped to look more carefully at the numerous white cards under the header APPLY FOR A HOME IN THE NEW TOWN NOW.

All the properties advertised there seemed to be located in the New Town.

A face appeared above the ledge at the back of the window. Bernard knew it at once. Dr. Fisher! The good doctor had looked after the family's health for many years when Bernard was a boy. Bernard was startled. Dr. Fisher smiled, but the smile did not suggest either surprise or special interest. It was the formal, polite smile of a shopkeeper, detached and automatic, scarcely the greeting of a long-lost acquaintance. But Dr. Fisher had been a trusted family friend. One had chatted confidently and intimately with him about personal matters. The face disappeared. Ah! Dr. Fisher was going to make amends for his casualness. No doubt he would come to the door with the welcome of an old friend. But no: he didn't.

Feeling a little hurt, Bernard decided to move on, and he cast a last rather sad glance at the window. There it was again, Dr. Fisher's unforgettable face smiling at him over the polished oak ledge behind the show boards—the same oval glasses, the smooth graying hair. Bernard smiled in return this time, raising his eyebrows interrogatively as you do when you expect a response from someone—"*Ah! How nice to see you again. We must have a chat. How are you?*" But Dr. Fisher's expression did not change. The smile was amiable but unresponsively remote.

Bernard frowned, looked down, pondered, then looked up to see that Dr. Fisher had again disappeared. Would he come to the door this time? No, he didn't. Bernard shifted his feet impatiently. He had no wish to waste his time exchanging meaningless grins with faces in shop windows, even faces that had once been securely attached to well-liked personalities. But curiosity triumphed. He took hold of the brass door handle, pushed open the shiny black door, and then went through a second door, labeled GODFREY AND SON, ESTATE AGENTS, INQUIRIES.

The little office was paneled and furnished in polished oak. The countertop was bare, but there was a bell push in the right-hand corner, and someone had stuck a piece of white card under it with the message, PLEASE RING. Bernard looked around. There was little else in the room to break the monotony of polished oak except something that looked like a calendar on the wall behind the counter. The green cardboard front had gilt lettering stamped on it, GODFREY AND SON, NEW HOMES AT GIVEAWAY PRICES, but the tear-off sheet underneath it did not bear a date. A memo pad, apparently.

Bernard rang the bell. Promptly Dr. Fisher emerged through the door at the other side of the counter, sat down on a high stool, and faced Bernard.

"Hello, Bernard."

"Hello."

"What can I do for you?"

"Oh." Bernard was nonplussed. "So you run this place, do you?"

"That is so, Bernard." The doctor's head and shoulders bowed graciously.

Bernard's eyes drifted down over Dr. Fisher's dark suit. That a medical man should turn estate agent was perhaps not incongruous here. The services of the medical profession could scarcely be required on this side of the grave. No doubt practitioners would have to seek other, and perhaps humbler, fields of employment. One must not embarrass the doctor by a show of surprise.

"It makes sense, anyway."

"Good. I'm glad to hear it."

Bernard frowned. The tone carried a note of correction even though it was laced with good humor. What was Dr. Fisher's real status here? Surely Godfrey and Son didn't set up expensive offices so that their employees could discourage potential customers with their cool formalities.

"You're seeking a home?"

The quiet suggestion was voiced in a tone near incantation, sounding almost liturgical; as Dr. Fisher spoke, he held up his hands, palms inward, in a seemingly ceremonial pose, as though he were conducting a solemn church service.

It was then that the light dawned on Bernard.

Dr. Fisher was no doubt avoiding a too friendly and natural relationship because he was intent on bringing off a good business deal.

"What are you offering?" Bernard sat down confidently on the polished oak chair provided for clients.

Dr. Fisher bent down under the counter and lifted into view a great leather-bound volume, the size of an enormous encyclopedia, with a red band on the spine. The gilt lettering stamped on it read NEW TOWN. The doctor laid the great book on the counter and turned the pages reflectively. Lists of properties with attached photographs filled the pages, but he didn't seem to be looking for any particular property in which to interest Bernard. Maybe he was meaning to draw attention to the size of the market.

"It seems to be a buyer's market, Dr. Fisher."

"All markets are, Bernard. That's the nature of markets. But it isn't always easy to buy."

"It isn't always easy to sell either," Bernard said, feeling that bargaining was about to begin.

"Indeed. I don't know which is costlier—to buy or to sell. The purchaser may spend all, but the vendor sometimes pays a higher price."

Baffled, Bernard reached a quick decision. To think of competing with Dr. Fisher in uttering obscure repartees was just not an option. He plainly knew all there was to know about the techniques of verbal mystification. It was time to get down to brass tacks. He leaned over the counter confidentially.

"You'd like to sell me something, Dr. Fisher?"

"I'd like you to have a good home, Bernard."

"Same thing, I suppose."

"No. But never mind. You'll learn."

The tone of correction again. Was it perhaps a sign that Dr. Fisher was impatient now for talk of hard cash?

"What kind of money are we talking about, Dr. Fisher?"

"I know of only one kind, and actually, we were not talking about it. It's not the currency we use here in real estate."

Desperate for some clarity in negotiation, Bernard laid his hand on the book.

"Which of the properties in particular would you recommend to me?"

"A question impossible to answer, Bernard. All the properties are equally to be recommended."

"All equally desirable?" Bernard smiled knowingly, for it seemed that Dr. Fisher had once more resumed the role of salesman.

"All equally and totally desirable."

Bernard laughed, laid hands on the great book, and turned it halfway around so that he could inspect its contents. "You make it rather difficult to choose."

Dr. Fisher's hands reached out briskly to pull the book back around again and shut it with a bang. "There is, of course, no question of choice."

The rebuke stung.

"We mustn't quarrel, Dr. Fisher."

"Of course not."

"But you must admit that it isn't easy to do business in these conditions." He pointed his finger at Dr. Fisher's hand, flat and firm on the closed volume.

"It's not meant to be easy, Bernard."

Bernard shrugged his shoulders. "Never mind, Dr. Fisher. Perhaps someday later we may be able to do a deal together." He rose to go.

"I hope so. Meanwhile, you'll be staying hereabouts."

"I'm not sure about that."

"I am."

"What do you mean?"

"Until you get a house in the New Town, you'll have to."

Dr. Fisher tapped the closed volume. Bernard turned firmly back to the counter.

"Look here, Dr. Fisher, what is all this about? You talk to customers as though you weren't interested in doing business. Yet you deal with vacant properties hereabouts."

"New Town properties. That's all."

"Why is that?"

"What would be the point of dealing in property elsewhere? Everyone wants a home in the New Town."

"Why? What's wrong with this place?"

"My dear Bernard, don't you know? Old Hertham is condemned. The whole region is scheduled as a clearance area. There's no long-term future here at all."

"But what a pity. It looks an attractive place in a way."

"It looks so."

"I certainly wouldn't have thought of it as a depressed area."

"You will before long."

"Then it's very sad."

"We all feel like that at times," Dr. Fisher conceded.

"And yet it must go?"

"Under the Regional Clearance Scheme."

"And is there no opposition to that among the people who live here?"

"Opposition?" Dr. Fisher seemed to weigh the word. "There is a vocal minority who would like to see Old Hertham recognized as a special development area. They have listed certain buildings as especially worth preserving. They have established a preservation trust and a heritage fund to raise money for repairs. But their idealism is ill-directed. It flies in the face of the facts. The Old Town has no future."

Dr. Fisher's fingers continued to dance playfully on the closed volume. Bernard found the man's confidence disturbing.

"If that's the case, I suppose I ought to start thinking about a house in the New Town myself."

"You'll think about it, Bernard. You're sure to."

Manager and client stared at each other in silence for a few moments. Bernard frowned. This wasn't getting him anywhere. Should he go away baffled? Should he give in?

"Dr. Fisher, you said everyone wants a house in the New Town."

"I did. Deep down that's what they all want. Of course, they don't all know they want it. Lots of them think they want to stay here, as you will soon discover."

Bernard wasn't sure he liked the way Dr. Fisher presumed to understand other people's minds and wishes better than they did themselves. Perhaps it was a lingering relic of the professional assurance he had cultivated as a medical man.

"Suppose I want a home there myself. What's the procedure for getting hold of one?"

Dr. Fisher laughed. "It's a little bit early to start talking of getting hold of one."

"There must be a way of setting the machinery in motion."

"There's a starting point, of course. You must get your name down on the Waiting List."

"Fine. I'm all for that."

Bernard leaned over the counter. Dr. Fisher bent down behind it and placed the large volume somewhere in the depths. Then he straightened up again, holding a different large leather-bound volume in his hands. Bernard was dismayed to read on the red

16

section of the spine not only WAITING LIST but also the inscription A TO C.

Dr. Fisher riffled through the pages of the vast volume as if anxious to convey how extensive the List was. Bernard was flabbergasted to catch sight of columns of names packed together as in a telephone directory.

"You mean to say that these are all applicants for houses in the New Town?"

"Surnames A to C," Dr. Fisher said, closing the book and tapping the spine.

"It looks as though I'd better join the queue as soon as possible."

"Yes, you'd better."

"Put me down at once."

"Oh, I can't do that. You'll have to submit a formal application to be put on the List."

He bent down again and produced a wooden box, polished oak again. He took out a key from his pocket, unlocked the box, and opened it. It was full of forms that looked vaguely like the application forms for driver's licenses. He handed one over.

"You must fill in one of these, Bernard."

"No problem. I'm a habitual form filler."

He glanced at the sheet with its demands for such obvious particulars as name, male/female, date of death.

"It looks straightforward enough."

"At first sight it does."

Bernard looked at the form more closely.

"That's right, Bernard. It's important to read the small print."

Before this application can be formally considered, three references must be submitted to a registered agent. When these have been accepted, the names of references should be entered in the spaces provided below. Applicants can assume that a reference has been accepted unless they are officially notified otherwise.

"References?" Bernard queried.

"Yes, personal references testifying to your fitness to be put on the Waiting List."

"What sort of people can I get them from?"

"People who know something of you and can give a fair judgment on your character and reliability."

"But where shall I find them?"

"You'll meet them, Bernard. You'll run into them. Of course, it may take time, but there's plenty of that hereabouts. It doesn't run out up here, you know. And anyone whose name is already on the Waiting List is entitled to give a reference. That's the crucial qualification for a reference."

"I see," Bernard said weakly, feeling depressed.

Dr. Fisher leaned over the counter and laid a hand on Bernard's arm.

"Don't be dispirited, Bernard. I shall always be ready to help you. You have only to come here and see me at any time you like. Meanwhile—"

"Meanwhile," Bernard interrupted him, "perhaps I'd better take a look at this New Town."

Dr. Fisher shook his head forcefully, then bent down, took out a leaflet from under the counter, and handed it to Bernard.

"I'll give you one of the firm's cards too," he added, laying one on the counter.

At that moment an unseen buzzer suddenly set the room vibrating. Its effect was to transform the atmosphere and to galvanize Dr. Fisher. He pushed his hand under the counter, and the noise stopped immediately. He jumped off his stool, saying, "Excuse me," then stood up, looked out over the edge of the window, and assumed the same pose with which he had first greeted Bernard.

Bernard glanced at the leaflet in his hand:

ACCESS TO NEW TOWN

Residents of Hertham (formerly Hertha Magna) are well aware of the gigantic ravine, known as the Great Earthfall, that slices through the countryside a few miles east of Old Hertham. No one today questions the wisdom of the decision made long ago to site the New Town on the farther side of this ravine, well away from the area of decay now due for clearance.

The construction of the suspension bridge across the ravine was an immense feat of engineering. This bridge, known after its donor and designer as the Christopher Godfrey Memorial Bridge, remains the only route for travel between the Old Town and the New Town. It must be kept open at all times for official traffic. Unauthorized use of the bridge cannot be permitted. Authorized residents and those with official business in the New Town can obtain permits from the usual agencies.

Not greatly enlightened, Bernard picked up the card from the counter:

GODFREY AND SON

ESTATE AGENTS

MARKET STREET—OLD HERTHAM

Godfrey and Son is a family company long established in the Old Town and dealing in real estate but specializing in properties in the New Town. The firm is proud to have been originally established under the patronage of Sir Alph Godfrey, founder of Hertham. It was of special concern to Sir Alph that the best New Town housing should be made available to Old Town residents. To that end this OT agency for NT properties was first opened. The present proprietors remain deeply grateful for the special privilege of being allowed to continue to work under Sir Alph's name and that of his son, Christopher Godfrey.

> For further assistance at any time, call the Christopher Godfrey Helpline:
> Freephone NT 13579246810.

"I'm sorry about the interruption, Bernard. That buzzer makes a beastly noise, doesn't it?"

"Some kind of telephone?" Bernard asked.

"Not exactly. It's the electronic warning system. Someone was looking in the window with special interest. The video system picked him out. When you get that degree of attention from a passerby, it's important to show a corresponding interest. We're supposed to respond, you know—nothing pressing or compulsive, but just the friendly eye. It helps, especially with newcomers. They need encouragement."

Bernard was about to observe that they needed enlightenment

too, for the leaflet in his hand about access to the New Town raised more questions than it answered, but Dr. Fisher remained standing as though the interview was at an end, so Bernard rose to his feet again, and Dr. Fisher stretched out his hand.

"Thank you for your help, Dr. Fisher."

"Good-bye for the present, Bernard. You'd better have one of these."

He handed over what looked like a small visiting card and then disappeared through the door behind the counter.

Bernard turned to go, and marveling at the doctor's seeming enthusiasm for distributing bits of literature, he glanced at the little card in his hand.

OLD HERTHAM

RESIDENT INHABITANT PERMIT (RIP)

GODFREY AND SON

*How Bernard came to stay at Netherhome Lodge with Eve
Knight and her daughter, Marie*

Out in the street, Bernard suddenly felt very silly. Here he was,
a stranger in a very strange place, and he had no base, nowhere
to eat or sleep, and no idea where to turn for practical help. Yet
he had just spent half an hour or so in the company of an old
friend who was an established resident in the place. Why hadn't
he raised with Dr. Fisher a single one of the pressing practical
questions that face a newcomer? Had the man mesmerized him?
Why on earth had he let himself get involved in a long rigmarole
about a hypothetical future home in a never-never land?

He strode past the shops and offices, feeling that he ought to kick
himself. The briskness of his walk said what he felt. A dog shakes
the drops off its back when it leaves the water. He had to shake
himself free like that, free of the unreality permeating the inside of
Godfrey and Son's office. What was the respectable medical man
supposed to be doing there? Who did he think he was, with his
precious directories and his battery of fussy regulations? Were the
other estate agents as bad as Godfreys'? There was one on his right
now, an impressive one in a grand building with a pillared classical
facade: PETERS UNIVERSAL AGENCY—THE OLDEST FIRM IN THE BUSINESS.

Its windows offered, FIRST-CLASS HOMES IN THE NEW TOWN—ALL STONE-BUILT AND OF TRADITIONAL DESIGN. And he could just see across the road to his left a smaller office jammed rather uncomfortably between two large stores: J. WESLEY & CO—THE AGENT WITH THE PERSONAL TOUCH—WE HAVE AN NT HOME FOR YOU.

Looking down a side street, he saw scaffolding around one building, and another had been buttressed, seemingly against collapse. Farther along the main street, he came upon an area of major damage. A vacant square of land with piles of rubble and gaping holes in the ground had been surrounded by barriers. Notices read DANGER—KEEP OUT, and there was a broken sign: TROY TOWER. This was the worst evidence of dereliction Bernard saw, and it was like a postwar bomb site. Otherwise, the degree of repair work apparently going on hereabouts did not seem all that remarkable. What he saw scarcely matched Dr. Fisher's picture of a town in total decay.

"Bernard!"

There was a female voice behind him and a female hand on his back. He turned to meet an astonished face.

"Don't you know me, Bernard?"

It must be, Bernard thought. *But surely the face is too young.* Still he ventured, "Eve?"

"Of course."

"But you're the same age as me . . . I mean you should be."

"I was once, but I came here at twenty-eight. So that's my age now."

"You mean we keep the age we had when we died?"

"That's right."

"Forever?"

24

"I don't know about that."

"How terrible. I shall always be twelve years older than you here."

"It isn't terrible at all. It's fun when you get used to it. Take Marie, for instance. That's my daughter. She died eleven years after me. Same thing, you know—a car crash. Roger finished the two of us off, wife and daughter in turn. And he's still going strong down there."

"I know, I know," Bernard said, doing his best to pull the right kind of face. "It was tragic."

"Not really!" Eve still spoke gaily. "Though I was a bit peeved over one thing—all they did was to mark his driver's license for killing me, but they took it away for twelve months for killing Marie. So unjust to me, don't you think?"

Bernard shook his head. Whatever were the right words for such tidings?

"But what was I telling you? Oh yes. Marie was twenty when Roger crashed into the back of a truck. He'd been drinking, of course. So I have a daughter here just eight years younger than I am. And you can have funnier things than that."

Eve's eyes seemed to sparkle girlishly as they had years ago when she and Bernard were both seventeen. What would Marie be like? An exact replica of the Eve he had lost?

"Have you only just got here?"

"Scarcely an hour ago."

"How wonderful for you! It's so exciting at first. I just loved it. What have you done?"

"Nothing, except I had an odd sort of interview with an estate agent."

The sparkle and the vitality died out of Eve's eyes and face. It was as though she had been struck suddenly by an unseen hand. Her head fell. She fumbled in her handbag, took out a handkerchief, and dabbed the corners of her eyes, half turning away.

"What's the matter, Eve? You're not ill, are you?"

She pulled herself together and swung around.

"Nothing at all. I'm all right, Bernard." She breathed deeply and stared up into Bernard's face. The sparkle was recovered as quickly as it had been lost.

Bernard searched her eyes. The brief evidence of unease reawakened his old tenderness for her. He began, "I thought for a moment—"

"Let's talk about you, Bernard," she interrupted with a forced brightness. "Where are you going now?"

"How am I to know?"

"Where are you staying, then?"

"Same answer."

"Then you can come and stay with us. How lucky that I met you. You must come, Bernard, you must. Otherwise those people at the Newcomers' Advice Bureau will put you in one of their awful temporary bed-and-breakfast dumps."

She put her hand on his arm. Bernard could feel the tremor of her eagerness.

"At any rate, come and see whether you would like to."

Before he had time to reply, she had drawn him into walking at her side. Chattering all the time, she guided him along the pavement, thick with pedestrians, and across a busy road at some traffic lights, then tugged at his arm to pull him onto a side road. She hurried him forward, but at certain points he cast

26

his eyes down side streets and fitfully began to wonder whether Dr. Fisher's picture of a decaying fabric might have some foundation after all. For at several points he caught sight of ladders and scaffolding against buildings that looked as though they had been damaged in air raids or in an earthquake. Then too, the frequent warnings of ROAD WORK AHEAD and the railed-off workings reminded him of areas at home where water pipes and drainage were being renewed.

The road opened out, and it was not long before Eve and Bernard were walking between spacious grass shoulders.

"This is the best area of Hertham to live in, Bernard. It's open and fresh up here, much better than down near the river. And it's fresher still farther up. You'll love my cottage. It's got everything."

Bernard was soon able to appreciate what she meant. Netherhome Lodge had paneled walls and ceilings, deep-set windows, and polished slate fireplaces in a rich sea green. From some windows there was a view over open country to a rugged line of mountains. As Eve prepared a meal, Bernard took a look around the garden. It held a delightful little two-story building. The bottom story was a summerhouse, the upper story a little spare bedroom with a balcony outside the French doors. In contrast with the cottage, a solid-looking building, the summerhouse-cum-bedroom was Italianate and seemingly designed to be flooded in Mediterranean sunshine. Bernard stared at the green tiles on the square roof, the wrought-iron rails of the balcony, and the curved iron staircase. Pure Zeffirelli. It might have graced a scene in either *Cav* or *Pag*.

When Eve called him into the dining room for supper, Bernard had a shock. There, standing beside the Eve of twenty-eight, whom he had never really known, was the young Eve he'd lost years ago.

"This is Marie. Don't you think she's like me?"

Bernard could only nod in reply. Mother and daughter were like sisters. Eve's black hair was swept back into a bun, while Marie's was short and clustered about the ears, but profiles and features were astonishingly alike. The same brown eyes, same irresistible emphasis at the tip of the nose, same indescribable lift in the curve of the upper lip. Yet Bernard had to remind himself that the one on the right, the older one, was the woman he had known, the one at whose side he had walked and talked by the hour. The other woman was seeing him for the first time.

"If only I had some of my old photographs here so you could look at them side by side with Marie, I'm sure you would agree that she's exactly like I was at that age. You ought to know, Bernard."

"I don't need any photographs."

"I knew it." Eve's tone was as bright as ever. "You're quite overcome. She's me all over again, isn't she? Couldn't you just fall in love with her, Bernard? Everybody does, you know."

"Everybody?" Marie said quietly, and the way she said it made her sound somehow older, not younger, than her mother.

At supper Bernard was too busy savoring the personalities of the two women to comment on what he was eating, enjoyable though he found it. He was made aware that he had overlooked some requisite courtesies when Eve prompted him.

"Did you enjoy it, Bernard?"

"Delightful."

"I know how fond you are of roast ham and salad."

"You do?"

"Bernard, don't you remember?"

"Remember what?"

"Surely you haven't forgotten the Lamb and Flag?"

Frantically Bernard groped for a clue.

"You know, the inn at Oldbiggin, that day with Jim and Vera."

It all came back with a rush, the debris of the past suddenly deposited on the surface of Bernard's consciousness as by a tipping truck: a sunny July day, a bus ride out to Oakley, a walk over Strothdown Moor, he and Eve sitting on a wall, waiting for the slightly older couple to catch up—Jim, red-faced and sweaty, just that little bit too plump for moorland rambling, and Vera, always and everywhere all sensuous roundness and smiles, all polish and smoothness. It was teatime when they halted at Oldbiggin, turning into the Lamb and Flag, a solid tower of an inn, gray and somber on the gaunt hillside. Vera and Jim and Eve each had a modest afternoon tea with thin-sliced bread and butter and jam, but Bernard called for the high tea menu and kept them waiting and laughing as he made his way through a mountainous plateful of cold roast ham, potatoes, and salad.

Bernard had never been back to Oldbiggin since, but he could picture it now with a clarity that seemed to make his eyes ache as his mind rummaged among the fragments of the past.

"That was the day, Bernard, when my father was cross with me for being away so long with someone he didn't know. I suppose he was worried about me. What was I? Sixteen? A girl changes so quickly at that age. He must have felt he was going to lose me. And then, after all, he didn't lose me, Bernard, did he? Not to you, anyway."

"Not to me," Bernard said colorlessly, wondering whether Eve wanted him to express regret.

"Hear how calmly he says it, Marie? Who would think that he might have been my husband? Would you have liked him for a father? No, I think you prefer him as an unrelated friend, don't you?"

There was no reply.

"He's kept his charm, hasn't he? You wouldn't think he was over forty."

"Exactly forty," Bernard said.

"Something like that, anyway."

There was a pause, and then Marie spoke.

"I think he's patient," she said.

"He must have learned lots of patience," Eve said laughingly. "He went on to spend his days teaching Latin to youngsters who probably had no wish to learn it. Can you think of anything duller? Maybe there were compensations for him, reciting *amo*, *amas*, *amat* to nubile high school girls and sorting out their genders for them. I expect he used the direct method for that. I can just picture it."

Bernard cringed. Surely the young Eve he remembered had had much more of Marie's calm and stillness, much less of her present forced brightness and chatter.

After supper they moved into the sitting room, a long, narrow room with two windows looking out across the road and toward the hills and a fireplace at the narrow end. Bernard admired the color scheme—the salmon carpet, the rust-toned upholstery, the green slate of the fireplace, the flushed ivory of the wall panels. He was commenting to Marie on Eve's good taste when Eve herself brought the coffee in. The smell of it was enough to put the finishing touch to a scene of delightful homeliness. And the sight of Eve, bare armed, with her fawn blouse and chocolate skirt, gently easing her way between the armchairs, fixed Bernard's gaze.

Then the dreadful thing happened. Eve shouted, her leg seemed to crumple up beneath her, the tray tipped, the cups and saucers clattered and slithered, and a quarter of a second later there seemed to be scarcely a surface in the room that was not stained and dampened by coffee, littered with fragments of broken china, or stickied with sugar. Bernard bent down to Eve.

"Eve, are you hurt?"

"No," she said, leaning heavily against him.

He helped her to her feet. Then, when she saw what a mess she had made, she burst into tears and sank down on the arm of a chair, covering her eyes with her hands.

"Eve!"

"It's ruinous, ruinous. The carpet, the chairs, the walls, everything!"

Bernard put his arm over her shoulder.

"We can soon clear it up, can't we, Marie?"

"What's the use?" Eve shook her shoulders and sobbed. "It will happen again."

31

"Why should it? You tripped on the wrinkled-up carpet, that's all."

"I didn't."

Bernard appealed silently to Marie, who stood there collected and undemonstrative.

"It's the floor," she said. "Let me show you."

Under Marie's guidance Bernard pushed the chairs clear and rolled back the carpet. Underneath, a floorboard had snapped in the middle and given way. Bernard lifted up the fragments. They were rotten, and the joists underneath were soft and pulpy and smeared with a pinkish white fungus.

"It's dry rot. You ought to have this attended to."

"What's the good?" Eve sobbed.

"You can't get it dealt with," Marie said quietly.

"Why not?"

"Because of the Regional Clearance Scheme. The whole of Old Hertham is a registered clearance area where you're not allowed to do anything other than inexpensive minor repairs."

"Then you should move to another house quickly."

Marie shook her head. "Half the houses in Hertham have dry rot, and those that are free of dry rot have something else nearly as bad—death-watch beetle or woodworm or crumbling roof tiles."

"If that's true, Marie, then the whole thing is a scandal. I mean, it should be dealt with. The problem should be tackled on a big scale. It's vast."

"An epidemic of decay," Marie said.

"Surely the powers that be are going to do something about it."

"There's the New Town. They're building it all the time."

"While this place rots." Bernard shook his head.

"If they were to rebuild here or to repair these houses properly, then it would all take from the labor force working on the New Town. That's what they always say. There's a limited amount of building material available too. They don't want to waste it."

"It surely isn't a waste to ensure that people can live without holes under their feet." Bernard was genuinely indignant.

"Oh, they'll let you patch up a bit, just enough to keep going."

"Until the house gets just too bad," Eve said.

Bernard looked at her, a beaten huddle of sagging shoulders and limp arms.

"I think it's monstrous," he said.

Marie shook her head. "It's logical. What would be the point of wasting effort, trying to give a false permanence to something that can never last?"

"These houses have to be lived in."

"For the time being."

"And they're not fit to be lived in."

"They're not fit to make a settled home in, but they're good enough to stay in until a proper home is available."

"And when will that be?"

Neither of the women answered.

"Haven't you got your names on the Waiting List?"

Eve's shoulders began to shake.

Marie put her finger to her lips. "It's a sore subject. I think we'd better tidy up. You go and rest, Mother."

Eve seemed glad of the excuse to go. Marie fetched a pail of warm water and some rags, and within half an hour she and Bernard, crawling around the room, had collected the debris, rubbed the stains from the carpet, spooned sticky sugar from a chair, and detached the buttered crackers from the hairs on the rug. Then they sat down together, and their eyes met.

"That's that, Marie."

Marie nodded. The hint of a smile lifted her lip, and suddenly both of them were smiling.

"I suppose it just had to happen tonight, Bernard. It's a shame. Mother just bought this carpet only recently."

"We shouldn't laugh, then."

"No . . . but what else is there to laugh at?"

Bernard lifted his eyebrows in silence, sharing her question. Then, lowering his eyes, he studied the floor, ruminating.

"Your mother is pretty sore about the Waiting List, isn't she?"

"I'm afraid so. She tried pretty hard to get herself put down on the Waiting List when first she came, and eventually she tracked down a man who had been one of the governors of her old school. He was a learned man, a professor of sociology or something. Mother wrote to ask him for his help, and of course, she made the standard formal enquiry: 'Are you qualified to act as reference for a person seeking residence in the New Town?' Professor Simpkins replied that he was. Mother showed me the letter. 'No one is more fitted than I for such a privilege,' he wrote, and he sent her a reference immediately. Mother was delighted. She gave a party for her friends, and they all drank her health. But there was a terrible letdown. Professor Simpkins was not on the Waiting List himself. The policeman brought back the original reference with a circle round the professor's name. It was rubber-stamped NOT KNOWN HERE.

"Mother was heartbroken. She couldn't face her friends for weeks. The experience has made her bitter. Unfortunately, she doesn't blame Professor Simpkins. She blames the authorities. 'What can you make of the powers that be if they have no respect for a learned professor who was well-known on TV?' she says. I don't think she should talk like that. Rebelliousness of that kind doesn't do you any good here. I've always found the agents helpful. Dr. Fisher was our family doctor."

"Was he? He was ours too. I'm told he delivered me."

"Me too. I like him. And he's worth knowing. He has close connections with the New Town. At times I've seen him driving in Hertham with one of those stickers on his windshield that says, NEW TOWN ENTRY—BCP. That's a bridge crossing permit. Very few people can get hold of those."

"Are you in touch with him?"

"In touch, yes, but not on the Waiting List yet. Listen, Bernard. It's my secret. I've got two references already. I only need a third. But you mustn't tell Mother—she's mixed up with the anti–New Town crowd now, and she gets very worked up on the subject. She's got a terrible resentment against the authorities. So please keep quiet about what I've told you. You must promise."

Bernard promised.

*How Eve sought to bewitch Bernard in the closeness of his
bedroom with recollections of their romance*

Marie showed Bernard to his bedroom—the spare room on top
of the garden's summerhouse. Delighted, he thought how this
arrangement would silence several half-formed scruples. He'd
wondered whether it was a good thing to live in the same house
as one's teenage sweetheart long married to someone else.

"You must feel like a dog sent out to kennel." Marie laughed
apologetically.

In fact, he felt relief. He bid Marie good night and thought
there was something uncomfortable about having the two women
close. Both, in their different ways, demanded attention. Eve
actively cried out for it, and he was compulsively drawn to
Marie—the woman he remembered from their youth.

Next morning Bernard was awakened by a surge of sunlight.
It flooded the balcony and seeped through the French doors
onto his bed. The curtains were parted a few inches in the
middle. If he lifted his head from the pillow, he could just
see the sky. Footsteps on the iron stairway leading up to his

room disturbed him. There was movement at the door, and Eve came in.

"May I? I've brought a cup of tea."

She was wearing a little apron over the skirt of a two-piece, formal ensemble, a combination that seemed girlishly out of synch. As she put down the tray on the bedside table, the full strength of her perfume flitted over to Bernard from her loose pink blouse. She went out onto the balcony while Bernard drank his tea.

She lingered there as he wondered whether she was intentionally giving him time to comb his hair and de-rumple himself.

"Heavenly!"

The call from the balcony seemed to imply an accompaniment of upturned face and outstretched arms. Bernard felt that some essential reticence was lacking. If you put your onetime boyfriend in a spare bedroom in the garden, you show a nice delicacy. If you then display yourself noisily on his balcony next morning, you somehow cancel out your delicacy.

When Eve came in again, she closed the curtains behind her back and held them as though she were taking a curtain call. Then she came over to Bernard, took his cup from him, and sat down at his side.

"Isn't it wonderful that we're together again, Bernard?"

"It's quite a surprise." Bernard spoke rather less gushingly.

She swung her legs onto the bed and leaned over toward Bernard as he lay there on his back staring uneasily at the ceiling. Her elbow dug into the pillow as she propped up her head in her right hand.

"Bernard, do you remember that trip up Yoredale to Eden Fall?"

"I remember."

"I think it was one of the most wonderful days of my life. What about you?"

Bernard was silent. He recalled a rare June day, blue and blinding, and a coach drive up the winding dale between the limestone crags and the shimmering river. The curate at their parish church was behind the planning of it, and there was a chattering communal tea in two farmhouse rooms, with huge plates of apple pie laid out on trestle tables. It was after the meal that he and Eve escaped the others. They scrambled down a steep bank through the thick tangle of trees and undergrowth, then came to rest at the riverside.

Suddenly liberated by the openness and the sunlight, they stood hand in hand on the warm rocks between the sheer blue and the glint of water. Eden Fall spread out at their side in a sheet of silver. It was just the right scene for what happened. Bernard held Eve and studied her eyes before kissing her lightly. *"Forever!"* he had said.

"I remember standing on the rocks and staring at the falls." Bernard's tone of voice was evasive.

"And afterward we lay down in the field, rather like this. Only I think you were a bit more responsive, Bernard." She dug her elbow into his side with a nervous laugh that seemed to deprecate what she was doing.

"We were young." Bernard tried to distance the memory. Being a teenager in the flush of a first romance was rather different from being a middle-aged pedagogue established in bachelor habits. There was a crucial distinction, too, between lying on the grass on a warm summer afternoon and lying in a strange bed, newly awakened from sleep, bleary-eyed and unshaven, early in the morning.

"We were genuine. You stayed genuine, Bernard. I didn't."

"Oh, don't say that." Bernard was embarrassed.

"That day you said you would always love me. Always."

He stared hard at the ceiling.

"You said 'always,' Bernard."

"It was you who broke it off."

"That's what I'm coming to. It left a loose end in my life. I've never managed to tie it up. Now I have the chance. At least I can say I'm sorry. And I mean it, Bernard."

"It's a bit late in the day, Eve."

"It's never too late." Her eyes wandered slowly over Bernard's eyes and head. "I admit that I let you down. That's what I want to explain to you." She drew several deep breaths as though she were on the point of sobbing.

Anxious to avoid a scene and to keep down the emotional temperature, Bernard lifted his hand and patted her on the shoulder. "Forget it, Eve. That's all done with."

"It isn't done. Not until I've explained. You see, it wasn't the real me that turned against you."

"Whoever it was bore a remarkable resemblance to you."

"Bernard, how can you, when I'm trying to explain? The real me got lost. That was the trouble."

"The real you went off to marry Roger, if I remember rightly."

"That was ages later."

"Less than two years."

Again the deeply drawn breaths, the hint of possible tears.

40

"I'm full of sympathy, Eve, and I'd hate you to be unhappy, but I can't see the point of going back to a past that was lost. For me, you're Roger Knight's wife. There's you . . . and there's a grown-up daughter, both decently buried down there and fondly remembered by a loving widower. They tell me he has a little commemorative plaque in his BMW to remind him."

"Bernard, you never used to be so bitter."

"Perhaps I hadn't cause. At eighteen I hadn't lived for twenty years as an adult bachelor."

"All that's behind us."

"You're still Roger's wife."

"Not here, Bernard. That doesn't matter here."

"There's such a thing as morality."

"Not here, Bernard, not of that kind. There are no rules about personal behavior here. Old Hertham isn't like that. The agents might like to think it is. And there are still lots of people who take notice of them. But we know better now. We don't have a mechanical list of dos and don'ts. We just know that we must respect ourselves and not hurt other people. That's what matters. After all, living honestly isn't a matter of following rules and regulations; it's really a matter of getting to know who you are. You have to learn to be you. That's what Professor Simpkins always says. I wish you could meet him."

"Simpkins!" Bernard was genuinely astonished. "Surely he's the fellow who deceived you."

The words came out before Bernard had time to realize that he was breaking a confidence.

Eve's eyes blazed. "You've been talking about me to Marie. What has she been telling you?"

"I'm sorry. I shouldn't have said that. Forget it."

"It's a lie." Eve now spoke quietly. "Professor Simpkins did the best he could for me. He gave me the most wonderful reference. 'I can recommend her with full confidence,' he said. 'No waiting list would be complete without her.' He always puts things so beautifully."

"What he said didn't get you anywhere."

"That wasn't his fault."

"But he tricked you. His own name isn't even on the List."

"It ought to be. That's the trouble. He disagreed with the agents. He said what he thought about them. And then they got their revenge."

"At your expense."

"Listen, Bernard. Professor Simpkins is a man who takes the housing situation here seriously. He thinks that a secure home ought not to be a privilege for the few. It's everyone's right. He's deeply moved by the needs of the people around him. And he can't bear to see the agents pushing them around and frustrating them. He tackled the people at Godfreys' face-to-face, asked them what their authority was for the way they run the housing allocations. Of course, they shut up like clams then. But he stuck to his guns and attacked them publicly in the *Hertham Gazette*. He just doesn't believe that access to the New Town should be rigidly controlled by professional agents with all their formal rules and regulations. He believes in people. He believes we all have to be true to ourselves and not slaves of anybody else's notions of what is proper. And that's what matters, isn't it, Bernard? You and I know that."

She leaned closer over him.

"You and I know that," she repeated slowly, and she lightly put her lips to his head.

He had a comic vision of himself as Beatrice Potter's Tom Kitten being rolled up in pastry to make a pie. It seemed quite impossible to respond with any warmth. He would have to be brutal in order to be kind.

"All I know is that I should like to get dressed," he said.

Eve pulled herself together, jumped off the bed, and left without another word.

How Bernard began to love Marie, and a mischance that befell them

If only it had been the other way around! If only the daughter were offering herself instead of the mother! Bernard was tormented by the irony. Wherever he might look in the cottage now, there in his mind's eye stood Marie. She was the real Eve he had loved. Her mother was the Eve who had shaken him off to become the wife of Roger Knight. That had ruptured their shared life. But there was no rupture dividing him from Marie. In appearance, in bearing, in the way she looked and spoke and laughed, she was the Eve he had made those promises to. Her mother might repeat the operative words to drag back the past—Oldbiggin, the Lamb and Flag, Eden Fall—but she could never renew the experiences they signified. Only Marie could do that. Those experiences could not be revived by a woman who had left him, humiliated him. Their meaning lay in the fact that the girl partner in them would be what she said she would be.

Eve was trying to do the impossible, trying to bring back those shared experiences to him after spending the rest of her life denying them. The experience of a trusting boy and a trusted girl could not be revived after the trust had been betrayed. No doubt all this would look different to Eve. She probably sensed no comparable alienation from him. It was possible for her to recapture the past in his presence, because he had never turned himself into a destroyer of that past. For her, he could still be the Bernard who had sat on the wall at her side at Oldbiggin and made promises to her at Eden Fall. For him, it was different. Eve's alienation of herself obtruded between the past and its reliving.

Was he being perfectly honest with himself? He asked because in different circumstances he might have questioned whether a man could respectably woo the daughter of a former sweetheart. But Eve was a married woman—and surely not really available. After all, he had known Roger personally, even if he hadn't cared for him very much. He didn't want to picture how Eve had passed the time between Eden Fall and Netherhome Lodge. It was enough to know that she'd had years of life with a husband while a daughter grew up from babyhood to become Marie. Meanwhile, he'd been listening to shoptalk among the teaching staff of Asgard School when he wasn't otherwise occupied with declensions and conjugations, with Virgil and Livy, with Ovid and Cicero. It wasn't that he hadn't enjoyed life in a way, but the smirks of those who thought he was homosexual because he was single hadn't been much fun, and being single had probably prevented him from getting that promotion. Sometimes, he suspected, even his own mother had wondered . . .

No, the parting of their ways put Eve way out of reach of his deeper sympathies.

This morning as they breakfasted, he couldn't help fastening his eyes on Marie. Did she know? Had she guessed that Eve had been with him? If so, she gave no signal.

Afterward he went out into the garden. "To take the air," he said, anxious to think things over.

It wasn't long before Eve came out and took her leave.

Bernard had been told that she had a part-time job at the hospital, but he'd been so little interested that the words never really registered. Only now did he wonder what need there could be for a hospital up here.

Minutes later, from the far end of the slate path that ran the length of the garden, he heard the cottage door close. He turned, and the next moment Marie was walking toward him. Suddenly the past came back with a blinding clarity. This wasn't a girl recently met for the first time who was walking toward him. Here was the lost Eve.

Bernard felt flung back in memory to a long-gone summer afternoon, a party in the Adamses' garden at Paradise Green. Eve had arrived there before him that day, and as he strolled from the gate to the lawn, she came walking toward him with just such a tentative placing of the feet, just such a tilt of the head. She was wearing a flimsy dress with a bold leaflike pattern, the material so thin, the sun showing off her curves.

Bernard suggested they should sneak away for an hour, and they did, across the fields, through Habel's farmyard, and around to where they could cool their feet in the stream that came rushing down from Mound Top. As the brook left the open field, it had to be piped alongside a cart track between old barns, so it was fed into a gulley through a stone trough. The sides of the trough curved around to a spoutlike outlet from which the water dropped into the gulley in a miniature waterfall. The serpentine shape of the trough had inspired locals to call it the Snake's Head.

Eve took off her shoes and put her feet into the water there to cool them. Then she stood up and grasped a branch of an overhanging tree to keep her balance. She inadvertently moved her foot onto a sharp-edged pebble and jerked her leg in pain, jumping back onto the grass. Bernard remembered her sitting there on the grass, waving her foot in the air and then stuffing a handkerchief inside her shoe because there was some blood on her heel. Today's reproduction of the lost one only said that she was going off to her work at the council office, and Bernard was left to his thoughts in solitude.

By the time Marie came back home in the late afternoon, Bernard had thought so long, hard, and lovingly about her that he wanted to pull her straight into his arms. But there were questions he couldn't answer. What did she know of Eve's visit this morning? What did the twenty-year age gap between Marie and himself look like from her side? It was hard to be plagued by such doubts, for she came back in a fresher and brighter mood than he had yet seen.

"It's turned very wet," she said, shaking her head. "And by the way, Mother will be late. She phoned me at the office. They've got some emergency cases to deal with at the hospital. It happens from time to time. Sometimes she's there all night."

Bernard's heart jumped with hope. But he tried to sound casual.

"What do you mean by 'emergency cases'? People can't die here."

"Oh no. It's a mental hospital. I thought you knew."

"No one told me."

"Sorry. There's so much to tell you. You know, Bernard, it may sound rather unkind, but I'm glad Mother is to be out this evening."

Bernard's heart jumped again. He moved toward Marie, hands already slightly lifted.

"You see, I've something special to tell you."

Bernard began to reach for her.

"But wait till supper is over," she said, swinging away into the kitchen.

They had their supper and their coffee, and no floorboards gave way this time. Of course, they were on their guard. They both avoided that patch in the middle of the sitting room, and Marie trod gingerly when negotiating the armchairs with the coffee tray.

She sat down at Bernard's side on the sofa.

"Make room for me," she said.

Her arm was in his ribs, her knees against his legs. She opened her bag, produced a long white envelope, and waved it in her hand.

"Reference number three!"

"Your last one?"

"Yes, I'm almost through."

"I'm so . . . glad . . . Marie." Bernard hesitated. "I think that's what you want me to say. Of course, I only want to say what you want."

"Don't you want to look at it?"

49

The edge of the envelope tapped his fingers. He took it, opened it, and read:

FROM THE REFEREND JOHN ABBOT
This is to certify that in my best judgment Marie Knight is a fit person to be enrolled on the Waiting List for residence in the New Town.
John Abbott

"You're sure this is valid?"

Marie pointed her finger at the heading of the certificate.

"I thought 'Referend' was a misprint," Bernard said.

"It means he's officially accredited by the authorities to issue references."

"So he's got his own name on the List?"

"Yes, but he's not pressing for a home in the New Town yet."

"He prefers to stay here?"

"He's one of those who believe that people here need the support and encouragement of individuals who already belong, heart and soul, to the New Town and can help by steadying people. There's so much worry and uncertainty and doubt in Old Hertham. These referends believe in encouraging people, teaching them to be patient, reminding them of what a lot there is to look forward to."

Bernard wanted to share Marie's seeming delight, yet he couldn't seem to find a way. "Now that you're on the Waiting List—"

"Oh, but I'm not," Marie interrupted. "Not yet."

"You've got your three references. Isn't it straightforward now?"

"Not quite. There has to be a hearing."

"A hearing?"

"Yes. Your name is published as being adequately recommended for the Waiting List, and a date and time are fixed for a public hearing. That's a sort of inquiry. Any people who object to your inclusion on the List have the right to attend and say why. If any of their objections are treated seriously by the inquiring officers, then your addition to the List is postponed until you have satisfied the authorities over the questions raised. Sometimes that can take quite a long time."

The words *long time* gave some secret comfort to Bernard. He turned now toward her and saw eyes dark and deep in the lamplight—Eve's eyes of twenty years ago. He took Marie by the arms. "Do you think I'm terribly old?" he asked.

"There's no age problem here, Bernard."

"Do you really feel like that?"

"It's not a question of feeling."

"Fact?"

Marie nodded.

"Does that mean I can kiss you?"

Without replying she threw her arms round his neck. The tightness of her clasp took him by surprise. The two of them sank sideways on the sofa in an embrace that seemed to promise an answer to all Bernard's long-frustrated hungers. But as their heads came to rest against the arm of the settee, there was a sudden scraping, slithering noise, and what felt like a bucketful of cold water came pouring down upon their faces, cracking against their cheeks with an unnerving, frostlike bite.

They jumped up. Bernard, shouting, thrust a handkerchief

into his eyes. Marie, whose hair dripped stiffly over the carpet, bent her head in silence.

"Holy smoke!" Bernard exclaimed.

"It's a bit cold for that," Marie said.

Bernard wasn't laughing. "What's it all about this time?"

"The roof. We've had this kind of trouble before. A slate must have slipped. And it happens to be raining."

"A slate! Half a dozen slates surely."

"Maybe. But I suspect it's just one slate from under the end of the gulley coming down from the two-story section of the house. The water is still coming in, though it isn't pouring any longer."

Bernard nodded vigorously. "So! The slates are all rotten too, I suppose."

"No. The slates are all right. The trouble is what the builders call 'nail weariness.' The nails that hold the slates in place are so old and rusty that they are beginning to give way."

"And they will go on giving way?"

"One by one."

"Delightful!"

"It has its funny side," Marie said, squeezing further drops from lank strands of hair.

"I'm rocking with laughter."

"I thought you were just shaking the water out of your ears."

"That too."

"It's clean water, anyway." Marie stared down at the dampened carpet.

"We hope so." Bernard wiped his eyes. "And I must say that there are occasions when the New Town sounds like a good idea."

"Agreed."

"Not that I approve of allowing a place to rot like this. Surely if the slates themselves are sound, it would be worth the price of a bag of nails to get your whole roof sound again."

"It's a bigger problem than that. The laths and the roof beams are too soft to take new nails. No, I can see the point of not allowing us to reroof the cottage. The rot is too widespread. There's a stage at which it's better to start again."

"You've been into it quite thoroughly?"

"Mother has. She tried to get a permit for reroofing, and the authorities sent an assessor around to make a full survey. His report left no hope. First, the nails are disintegrating; second, the laths and beams are too soft with damp to take new nails; and third, there is a weakness in the back wall. It's a bit out of true, and the stones are loose. Nothing immediately troublesome, they say; the wall is quite equal to present demands upon it, but if you tampered with the roof beams or tried to fit new ones, you'd be sure to dislodge more stones, and you could let yourself in for a rebuilding job on the walls."

"If I get your meaning," Bernard ventured, "tackle the nails, and you'll have to tackle the laths; tackle the laths, and you'll have to tackle the roof beams; tackle the roof beams, and you'll have to tackle the walls."

"That's what it amounts to. It was useless to think of appealing against the assessor's report."

Bernard's tone was heavily ironic, "He seems to have made an unanswerable case."

"Assessors always do. That's their job. They always prove houses unfit for major constructional overhaul by virtue of widespread decay."

"Meanwhile, the inhabitants of Netherhome Lodge must willy-nilly play their parts in a slapstick farce without the humor? Floors collapse under our feet? Bucketfuls of cold water drop on us from above? It's a terribly outdated scenario. We're back in the age of Laurel and Hardy. When do we start to throw the custard pies about? Perhaps we should wait for your mother to come back for that."

"I'm glad you can take it so cheerfully. Is my hair dry at the back?"

"Dry as silk," He said, smoothing it gently with his hands.

"Do that again."

"Well, take the towel away."

Marie let the towel fall to her shoulders, and Bernard held her for a moment quite still.

"I can't tell what you're thinking, Marie."

"I'm not thinking."

"Just waiting?"

"I didn't say so."

But the smile did. So he pulled her gently toward him and would have kissed her, but they heard the outer door open and Eve's voice greet them from the entry. "Hello there!"

"Thoughtful of her," Marie said, drawing away from Bernard as he dropped his arms in despair.

How Bernard made household repairs, and his encounter with a conservationist

As a male guest in a female household, Bernard felt he must try to help with the running repairs now so badly needed.

"Don't call in anyone to repair the floor or the roof. I'll see what I can do myself when you're both out at work," he told Eve. "I'm assuming that you have some tools somewhere. And is there any wood?"

"You'll find some things in the garden shed," Eve said, "but it's really a job for a handyman, especially the roof."

Bernard thought this might be something of a challenge, but one morning when left alone, he rolled back the carpet, measured the broken floorboard, and went to the garden shed.

He was lucky. There was wood and a saw; he was able to match the broken board exactly. He found some difficulty in fitting the new piece into place. The joists were soft on top, and there was a space where a completely rotten joist had given way. This space was at the point where one end of the new board should have been nailed to its moorings. If anyone were to jump heavily on the new floorboard there where the joist was missing, the board would probably be levered off the joist to which it had been nailed farther along its length. Then it would probably bounce right away from its moorings, coming up with a swing at one end and letting someone's foot drop down at the other end. It could cause someone to fall as Eve had fallen, and even more dangerously.

Yet the missing joist could not be replaced, so the risk had to be taken.

Bernard made the new piece as firm as he could. Then he tested the weak spot. First he tried half his weight on it, then his full weight. The board remained firm. He tried a light jump on it. He felt a slight springiness under his feet, but still the board held. He decided to let well enough alone. Why should anyone choose to leap about with special force on that one spot? Anyway, the thick carpet above it would distribute the force of any impact.

Bernard felt reasonably pleased with himself as he put the carpet back and moved the furniture into place. Then he turned his attention to the roof. Fortunately, it was not a dangerous roof to climb up to. The floor plan of the cottage was shaped like a letter *T*. The horizontal top of the *T* was a two-story building at right angles to the road. In that section there were bedrooms and a bathroom above the kitchen and the dining room. The vertical of the *T* was a one-story building parallel to the road. Here were the sitting room, the main entrance, a corridor, a utility room, and a coat room.

On the roof a gulley ran down the junction between the two-story and single-story sections. Its lead base was very narrow, yet it received the whole flow of rainwater from the roof of the two-story building on that side and carried it down the roof of the single-story section to the roof drains and downspouts. They had received that sudden downpour into the sitting room when a slate adjacent to this gulley first slipped.

Bernard used a long folding stepladder to get up and inspect the roof. In view of the general untrustworthiness of the fabric and especially the nails, he thought it best to distribute his weight while working rather than risk resting on any single slate at any one moment.

So he made a crude roof ladder, bound it to the top of the stepladder, and lay on it while working. It surprised him that the job seemed less difficult than he'd feared. The slate that had slipped was caught in the gutter but intact, and he was able to lift the slate above it just enough to nail the dislodged one back in place. He moved gingerly and worked carefully, making repairs without dislodging more slates—an achievement, he reckoned, as he got down. He surveyed the finished job with the comfortable feeling that he'd successfully walked a tightrope, then put the tools back in the shed.

He came out again to take in the folding stepladder. But it wouldn't pull away from the wall. He tried again, this time jerking it free.

The mistake was a fatal one.

The stepladder had come away from the wall—and brought with it a six-foot length of horizontal roof guttering and the vertical downspout that ran down the house at the junction of the one-story and two-story sections. Apparently, the steps had jammed themselves against the metal guttering when he'd put his weight on them. The guttering itself must have been feebly attached to the wall by iron pegs, and some of the pegs had rusted loose on the outer side; others had gradually worn free of the mortar into which they were socketed on the inner side.

The downspout must have been more firmly attached to the roof guttering than to the wall. Bernard found himself carrying the weight of a folding stepladder, roof ladder, guttering, and downspout, all detached from the building. His first impulse was to drop the burden in sheer despair. But something told him that such an unscientific response might create more problems than it solved.

Bernard gently backed away, moving his hand up the ladder and gingerly lowering the tangle of wood and metal to the earth. Before he could straighten his back and raise himself erect, a sudden frightening crash made him jump.

A new fall of slates lay heaped before him.

The mock-up roof ladder, which Bernard had corded to the folding stepladder, had scraped the bottom row of slates. The gutter must have helped hold these bottom slates in place, he realized. With the gutter gone, a quite light scraping by the roof ladder had been just enough to drag at the slates and snap the rusted nails that fixed them to the roof. As these slates slipped away, they landed on the downspout on the ground and splintered. Had they fallen on soft earth, he might have been able to reuse them.

Bernard groaned. What had been a small job now became a huge one, all the result of a trivial oversight—that light, thoughtless jerk on the jammed ladder. The damage would take days to repair.

Angrily he strode off to the garden shed to see what materials were available for possible repairs. There were no slates, and if it rained there would be a running torrent down into the sitting room.

He found a roll of roofing felt and cut a piece from it. He set up his stepladder again, propping it against the house with the sort of care and gentleness usually reserved for handling a newborn baby. He managed to stuff the edges of the felt under the slates adjacent to the gap, then came down to earth and stepped backward, watchfully eyeing his workmanship like a child waiting for a pile of bricks to collapse.

"The place is so strong that it will stand the additional weight of felt seemingly without sag or strain," he said aloud.

So the roof was waterproof again. Perhaps . . .

It looked a mess too.

What would Eve think? What hope was there of tidying up the damaged drainage before she came home that evening?

Actually, Eve arrived home at midday, and she had with her a stranger, a man in his midfifties.

Bernard, still trying to devise some sort of pegging to reattach the fallen downspout to the wall, stopped working.

Eve turned between Bernard and her companion. "I want you to meet Len Bollinge."

Bernard grasped at a limp hand. Len had the look of a kindly fish.

"He's secretary of the Old Hertham Preservation Trust."

"Oh, is he?"

"Bernard has only just come, Len," Eve explained.

Len nodded in sympathetic understanding.

"Quite. And I must tell him that this kind of thing is exactly what gets under my skin. Here you are, struggling to remedy a structural defect that ought never to have been allowed to develop. This beautiful old cottage should have been tended with loving care. But the authorities don't give a flip. They're quite prepared to let it rot."

"It's wicked," Eve agreed.

"Scandalous," Len corroborated.

"It is . . . frustrating," Bernard added.

"We're up against a bureaucratic machine that's quite ruthless," Len said. "We cannot make the authorities see reason. Many of the houses of Hertham are a priceless heritage from the past. Anyone who values what is beautiful must realize that a cottage like this is something to be cherished. The let-it-rot policy is sheer vandalism. Our society exists to strive by every means in its power to oppose the policy."

"Len's devoted to the cause," Eve added.

Len nodded with seriousness. "I'm a repairer and preserver, I hope, and am appalled at the modern craze for destruction."

"They say it would be costly to repair buildings like this properly," Bernard ventured, anxious not to appear too contrary. "I suppose there comes a point when it's better to start again."

Len shook his head ponderously.

"Len really does believe in the past," Eve explained.

"I sympathize with you in a way," Bernard conceded. "If I had limited labor and materials at my disposal, though, I'm not sure I'd want to use them to prop up buildings like this one. The place isn't really worth it."

Len shook his head again. "You can't measure the value of a home like this in terms of crude structural stability."

"You have to if you're a builder or a surveyor."

"Not if you also have a heart." The words seemed to come from some such place.

"Bernard is teasing you, Len." Eve laid her hand on his arm. "Let's all go inside and have a cup of tea."

She swung on Len's arm, and they went inside. Eve disappeared into the kitchen, and the two men chatted in the sitting room.

"You're not keen on the New Town?" Bernard asked. He realized what Len wanted to talk about.

"The New Town is all right in its place, but we've got to keep a sense of proportion. The New Town is way over there, and we're here. I can't bear those people who want to live mentally in that far-off place and meanwhile put up with appalling conditions here. 'After all, it's only temporary,' they say. That's all right in theory, but in practice we all know it's just wishful thinking. The Waiting List has reached a phenomenal length, and it's getting longer every day. They'll never catch up with the tremendous backlog of deserving applicants. And they don't seem worried either. The agents just go on encouraging people to apply. It isn't fair to trade on people's hopes as they do. And it isn't necessary. There are some fine homes here, all around us. They are worth preserving."

Eve came back with the tea. She put the tray down between them.

"Len is doing wonderful work, Bernard. We've got an open meeting of the Trust tonight with a special speaker, Professor Simpkins. You simply must hear him, Bernard. You would like to come along with us, wouldn't you?"

61

Bernard would have preferred to say, "No thank you." He didn't warm to Len, and he had no reason to think well of Professor Simpkins, but staring at him through the cottage window was the site where the broken downspout leaned against the wall. He was in an apologetic mood, feeling a special need to be nice to Eve after his miserable performance as an odd-job man. He acquiesced with a smile and a nod.

Soon afterward he had cause to regret his weakness. Just as they were preparing to set off for the meeting, Marie came home. There was a flush of excitement in her face—Bernard would have liked to call it anticipation—but it disappeared as soon as she heard that Bernard was going out with Eve and Len to the Trust meeting.

"Oh no," she said.

"Why not?" Eve turned on her.

Marie was silent. Len smiled indulgently.

In the awkwardness Bernard made a rather foolish effort at appeasement. "Aren't you going to come with us, Marie?"

"I couldn't bear it."

"She clings to other hopes," Len said with the air of a man explaining something. He seemed happy not to suffer from the same disability.

How Bernard attended a meeting of the Old Hertham Preservation Trust, and what befell him

Len drove Eve and Bernard to the meeting in his car. Bernard didn't look forward to the experience. However, having broken his hostess's guttering and punctured her roof, he felt that accompanying her was a small price to pay. Leaving Marie behind was a different matter. The consequences of his renewed acquaintance with Eve seemed to abound in ironies.

The chair was taken by a big-eyed lady who said that what they were about was terribly important, and wouldn't it be wonderful if everyone got together and put their hearts into it. Then, tapping the table in front of her, she stood up and said, "Old Hertham." Bernard thought at first that she was proposing a toast. But it was not so. The audience all stood up, a pianist struck a few chords, and everyone began to sing:

> And did those homes in ancient time
> Shelter from rain and wind and storm?
> And was Old Hertham builded here
> To keep its people dry and warm?

And did the authorities benign
Finance repairs to wall and roof,
Paying craftsmen double time
To keep the homesteads waterproof?

And have we now betrayed the trust
Of founding fathers, mothers too,
By letting damp and rot and rust
Invade the fabric, mar the view?

Bring me my book *How to Restore*
Period Homes of Every Age.
Give me the men, O crowds enroll
To save our precious heritage!

I will not cease from mental fight
In publishing our point of view
Till we've restored our dwellings here
And made Old Hertham new!

This formality over, the big-eyed lady introduced Professor Simpkins, a bearded, ascetic-looking man with a long, thin body and a head that rocked a bit. His subject, the chairlady said, was to be "Preservation: Its Wider Implications." She was delighted that he was going to direct their thinking outside their own backyards. "We mustn't be too parochial, or we shall become dull."

The professor nodded, and the audience murmured.

The prejudice against dullness appeared to be unanimous.

Professor Simpkins said much that was to be expected of a

guest of the Old Hertham Preservation Trust, much about the beauty and charm of Old Hertham and the need to preserve it like a precious jewel. But this sounded like courtesy stuff. The man's real enthusiasm showed through when he began to press the wider implications.

"I would go further," he said, stabbing a finger at the back of the hall. "We must preserve Hertham not only because it is beautiful but also because it is our home, our true home, the only home we can be sure of."

As he emphasized these words, here and there the audience noisily drew breath. Clearly, the professor had said something controversial.

"It is wicked to neglect the repair of Old Hertham on the fanciful grounds that labor and materials must be directed elsewhere for the building of supposedly more permanent homes," the professor continued. "Too many of our poor deluded fellow citizens accept the decay here because they are fed with the propaganda of the estate agents. Their hopes are kept alive by pie-in-the-sky promises of dream homes in the New Town beyond the canyon. But what reason have we for trusting the estate agencies in this respect? These charming gentlemen tuck themselves away in absurd little offices, surrounded by polished oak furnishings and leather-bound volumes that reek of dead tradition. What an absurd pantomime it is, the way they quote regulations and issue forms, the way they collect references and arrange hearings. Surely all this nonsense is pathetically irrelevant to the daily life of Hertham today. While these agents amuse themselves with their dead formulas and incomprehensible procedures, Hertham is rotting away and the Waiting List grows ever longer."

There was increasing passion in the professor's voice and a faraway look in his eyes.

"No dream of a New Town 'over there,'" he said angrily, "should be allowed to weaken our first loyalty to the place that is our present home. Why can't we have a permanent Hertham here, with all its ancient charms lovingly preserved and the best modern techniques applied to that task? Why are the agents so fanatically convinced that demolition must precede reconstruction? They are wrong! We have everything here that the heart could desire, if only we're prepared to cherish it.

"I ask all members of the Old Hertham Preservation Trust to urge their fellow citizens to look realistically at the world in which we live. We can only deplore the attitude of those victims of the agencies' propaganda who have managed to get themselves on the Waiting List. They strut about with their heads in the air, calling themselves 'Waiters.' They go around with grins on their faces just because they've been enrolled. Their complacency is laughable, their smugness repellant. They seem to think that collapsing roofs and rotting floors are nothing more than a joke. Their naïve trust in the Waiting List cuts them off from sympathetic contact with the real world around them. You see them with their heads buried in agency brochures, staring at glossy pictures of New Town houses. The real day-to-day practical problems we each face in our decaying houses seem to mean nothing to them. Mention these matters, and the Waiters start chattering vulgarly about dream houses in the New Town. Like the agents, they are forever going on about Sir Alph Godfrey and the wonderful society he is gathering around him in the New Town. They tempt people by pretending that new residents will be able to spend their time sucking up to Sir Alph and having a drink with Christopher Godfrey as though he could be everybody's best friend.

"The prime duty of the Preservation Trust surely must be to attack the escapism and obscurity of the Waiting List mentality. It is this mentality that stands in the way of concerted action against the Regional Clearance Scheme. As long as people succumb to New Town propaganda, they will accept like sheep the regulations that impede our work of preservation."

Professor Simpkins was impassioned now. "Everywhere," he declared, "Preservation Trust enthusiasts must combine to combat the propaganda of the estate agencies. We must focus people's minds on the here and now, the buildings about us, and the ground beneath our feet. On this ground we stand, here in Old Hertham. It is here that we must preserve, rebuild, and find our true security."

The conclusion had been flamboyantly put across, but the audience's applause was halfhearted. Were people apathetic? Or were they a bit frightened by the bold attack on the agencies?

"Most people are not ready for Simpkins's message," Len said as they drove away from the meeting. "It's too strong for them. They would like to preserve their homes, but they can't see the implications that follow. They are easily bemused by the agencies. After all, most people are conformists at heart. The system of allocating houses in the New Town has been operating for an awfully long time. People come here and get caught up in it. Few of them have the originality or initiative to question whether the system of selection for the Waiting List is any longer serving a useful purpose."

Eve turned to Bernard, sitting alone in the backseat of the car.

"Didn't you find the professor inspiring, Bernard?"

Bernard pursed his lips and said nothing.

Eve tried to coax him to respond. "Didn't you feel moved by the sincerity of his appeal at the end?"

"It was certainly cogent," Len said after a moment of continued silence from Bernard. "I liked those words about building on the home ground, the ground we're really sure of."

"Exactly," Eve said. "I found that most reassuring. He almost made me weep—"

A rumbling sound, like the roar of distant blasting, interrupted her.

"Whatever was that?" she asked.

The sound came a second time, louder, frighteningly louder, before it crescendoed into a sudden, thunderous, tearing noise all about their ears. Eve shrieked. The car jolted on the road, then lurched and seemed momentarily to take off in the air. For a split second they seemed to be in flight. Then came a jarring crash, pain in all their limbs, and a new blackness on every side.

"Good heavens!" Len cried.

Bernard struggled out of the car by pressing with all his weight against the jammed door. Then he tugged violently at the bent door that imprisoned Eve till he wrenched it free.

"Eve! Are you hurt?"

He bent over the sobbing, huddled mass, not knowing, in the darkness, whether she was whole or injured.

She was whole, and climbed out on his arm to stand up, shaking and shocked.

None of them had endured more than a great jarring of the flesh and bones and a sharp bruise to the nervous system; they were able to stand free of the car on their own legs.

"Where are we?" Bernard asked, staring into the darkness.

Len got back into the car and switched on the headlights. What at first seemed to be a wall in front of them turned itself into a jagged cliff, a sight that electrified Bernard.

Someone from above in the sky shouted, "Subsidence!"

Bernard searched above, finally realizing that a portion of the road about thirty feet long, the very portion they had happened to be driving along, had dropped at least eight feet. The car was neatly deposited in the bottom of what, to Bernard, felt like a vast natural grave.

"Anybody hurt?" the voice from above asked.

"No damage to us," Len shouted.

"We're bringing a ladder."

Within minutes a ladder was let down and a light shone from above. One by one Eve, Bernard, and Len climbed back to the normal road level. At the top they found a policeman and what looked like a fire engine.

"The car will have to stay there for the time being, sir. Have you far to go?"

"I can get a taxi," Len said, frowning at the officer.

"We two are almost home." Eve seized Bernard's arm.

"It might have been a lot worse." The policeman's tone was congratulatory.

Bernard thought he was taking it all very calmly.

How Bernard and Marie took counsel and solace of each other at Netherhome Lodge and in the hills

Next morning Bernard discovered that Eve had gone to the hospital and Marie had the day off. So as sun poured into the cottage, he sat with Marie, each on either side of a window overlooking the wide valley and low line of hills in the distance. Marie had made a jug of coffee and put it on the bamboo table between them. The comfort of it all seemed a far cry from the decaying fabric of Hertham.

And yet Bernard could not fully relax and forget it. Even his cheerfulness had an ironic flavor. He looked toward the ceiling and bathed his face in the sunlight. "So far, so good," he said.

Marie looked at him quizzically.

"If it doesn't rain, then we won't get drenched from above. And if we don't leap about too rashly, then we won't drop through the floor below."

"Now, now, Bernard. Gratitude please!"

"I'm counting my blessings. Didn't you hear me?"

"Oh, were you?"

"I was. And I got as far as two. Then I ran out."

"There must be lots more, surely. What about last night? Did you join the Preservation Trust?"

"Why should I?"

"Why should anyone?" Marie echoed.

"Right."

"We agree about that, then. Did you like Professor Simpkins?"

"Not much. Agreed again?"

"An orgy of accord. And what did the professor say?"

"He told us to build on the ground we're sure of, the ground beneath our feet. But it gave way on the journey back home."

"Oh no!" Marie rocked with laughter.

"About sixty square feet of it, I'd estimate. The very patch of road we were driving on dropped eight feet or so."

"What a scream! You must have laughed your heads off."

Bernard stared at her blankly. "At the time it didn't strike any of us as especially funny."

"But you make it sound like that."

"Do I? Then it's very selfish of me. Len must be taking a serious view of it all. You'll find his car at the bottom of a hole. Will they get it out, or will they bury it and run the new road on top of it?"

"That depends on how old it is and how damaged," Marie said solemnly. "It may be a write-off. The rule is that old, worn, or defective equipment, furniture, or machinery shall be buried and new, sound, and undamaged things shall be recovered. That is, if it can be done without too much effort or expense. I'm quoting the book, of course. And it's sometimes quite difficult to decide in borderline cases. There are regulations to help you, but they're very technical. When there's a problem, they always call in an assessor."

Bernard raised his eyebrows. "Are you serious, Marie?" He had thought he was making a joke.

"Of course."

"You mean there's a set of formal rules governing what happens to things when they drop down holes in the road?"

"There has to be. Subsidence is constantly occurring here. The whole area suffers from it. That's another reason why the authorities won't rebuild Old Hertham."

"Then Len may have lost his car?"

"Very probably. Whatever its condition to begin with, it must have been further damaged by the fall. It costs a lot to lift things back to ground level when subsidence has occurred. It's really not right to tie up scarce labor and expensive equipment in negative work like dragging debris out of holes in the ground. Sometimes half a house will drop, sometimes a bus or a truck. It would be so costly to try to recover them. A friend of mine had a concert grand piano in a rather small sitting room. She had trouble with floor rot complicated by a very slight subsidence. The piano dropped about six feet into the cellar. Even if they'd managed to get it up again, they would have needed a reinforced floor to support it. So they boxed the piano over."

"Surely that's a wasteful way of going on."

"It isn't, really. They're careful about anything really valuable. There's a scale of valuation set out in the subsidence regulations. It's called the recovery scale. An expert assessor can tell you in a moment whether something is recoverable. The police will probably call in an assessor to look at Len's car this morning, and they'll report to Len at once."

Bernard slowly shook his head. "What beats me is that this place should be officially organized on such a thorough scale to meet disasters like subsidence. It's all so pessimistic."

"Realistic, Bernard. That's what they always say. You can't legislate for an area subject to subsidence as though all the ground was firm. Sometimes people go down as you did. Sometimes they're lost in the depths."

"But the ground doesn't drop very far, does it?"

"It can. For the most part, it isn't a matter of purely natural subsidence, if there is such a thing. It's the old mines down there."

"Old mines? I didn't know."

"It's one of those things about Hertham that you gradually find out. The mining happened long ago, and nobody really knows the full history of it. There's quite a mythology on the subject. The agents will tell you the story of an ancient rivalry for rule in Hertha Magna, as it used to be called. Some rebellious spirit got too big for his boots and wanted to take over the running of the whole place. He collected a lot of malcontents. They plotted a rising, but they were exposed and Sir Alph banished them. The agents blame that lot for the decay of Old Hertham. It seems they were determined to get their own back and started to undermine the town, working from well outside the walls. They made a pretty thorough job of it, and the powers that be have never fully caught up with them."

"You mean they don't know exactly where the mines are?"

"It seems not. They don't appear to have charted the area and plotted the danger zones."

"Surely there must be the technology to do that."

"It's the old problem. Once the powers that be decided to write off Old Hertham and get as many of its inhabitants as they could into the New Town, there was no point in wasting resources on the old one. Christopher Godfrey came along, and he had the canyon bridged. Thereafter everyone's eyes were supposed to be focused on the New Town. That, at least, was the situation the agents really wanted."

"And they are the masters?"

"They've got their hands on the whole property industry. In the long run, they control everything."

"And they all stick together?"

"It's really a monopoly. The firms may have different names, but Godfrey and Son took them all over years ago."

"Why do people put up with it?"

"Because the agents argue that if they didn't hold the reins tight, the building of the New Town would come to a standstill. And whatever a few individuals might say, most people don't really want that to happen. They are afraid, especially since last year. When you left Godfreys' in Market Street, you must surely have caught sight of the damage done by the latest collapse. Troy Tower was the highest building in Hertham and the only really recent building in the whole town. They say the agents were against its construction. Be that as it may, the architects really went to town on it, and they had the Old Hertham Preservation Trust fully behind them. But when it came crashing down and men dug up the foundations, they found it wasn't just a case of what you might call accidental subsidence. Somebody had actually destroyed supports in the depths to make sure it came down."

"But how could they?"

"There's a network of underground workings down there, a vast labyrinth of passageways and caves. They reach out into the surrounding hills. Someone is still operating there. The agents call him 'the Old Enemy.'"

Bernard turned to study Marie's face as she gazed out toward the distant hills. Sun-washed and steady, her features carried that special air of tranquility that distinguished her from Eve. Her eyelids were half lowered against the sun's brightness, intensifying the sense that she was concentrating on something distant yet compelling.

"My dear!" he suddenly said. She looked up, smiling encouragingly. Her full face, searching his own, was again the face of Eve, bright under the light of a streetlamp as he said good night to her outside her home years and years ago. And yet . . . this was the face of an Eve image now obliterated in the curious reunion with her up here, the face of an Eve made wise and mature. How clearly he remembered her youthful clarity of line, the unspoilt freshness of it. He stood up, bent over her, and took her hands. She stood and turned to him.

"Marie, you're very lovely."

"If you say so," she said, smiling.

"You are very like . . . and yet very different from . . . your mother."

"So they tell me."

"You are so much younger than I am that I ought to ask you if you think me too old, but often I sense that you are somehow older than I am, and I feel I ought to ask you if you think me too young."

"You are beginning to talk like an agent."

"But it's true."

"Of course it is. Otherwise it wouldn't make you sound like an agent."

"You have your mother's hair and eyes and cheekbones." He smoothed them with his hand. "You are a little older than your mother was then, yet much younger—and perhaps older—than she is now."

"I think you've said enough to make your point," she said, laughing.

"Then can I take advantage of your age to take advantage of your youth?"

She did not answer but put her hands to his head, pulled it down, and lightly kissed him. Bernard thought this was a beginning.

But for the present, it was an end. She broke away, laughed, and took his hand firmly.

"Let's go for a walk."

"Must we?"

"*Must* is the word on a morning like this. I'll get a jacket. It won't be as warm as this away from shelter. Higher up, there's probably a cool breeze."

There was a breeze, but a mild one, as they climbed on a stony path past the last isolated cottage and onto an open, scrubby stretch of land. Their faces flushed with the warmth of exertion.

They stopped to rest where the path suddenly swept round to the right and crossed a stream with a rough bridge built of stone slabs. The stream curled down between the slopes of a glen into the river that eventually ran through Hertham. The glen was thinly dotted with trees and sheep and crisscrossed with stone walls; the slopes were broken by boulderlike crags jutting from the earth.

Marie took Bernard's hand and drew him off the track, onto the grassy margin, and up to a dry stone wall.

"This is the best spot for a view of the valley. I've tried them all, so I know."

She was just tall enough to see comfortably over the wall, and she rested her chin on the top tier of stones. Bernard stood for a moment at her side, his arm on her shoulder. Together they fed on the stillness and freshness of contours and color under a light blue, clean-washed sky.

Bernard felt the solace of a dozen remembered views. Among them were persistent images of the river Yore tumbling over Eden Fall and Eve standing at his side on the warm white rocks. He pressed Marie's shoulder, and she seemed to relax against him with a new willingness. He shifted position, moved behind her, and looked over her head, resting his chin on her hair as hers rested on the wall. They stood in silence then as he held her waist and smoothed her hair with his cheek.

"It's heavenly here, Marie."

"Yes."

"Turn around," he whispered. She did—a tight squeeze, jammed as she was between Bernard and the wall. Bernard was in no mood to make it less of a squeeze, and when she joined her hands behind his neck, he felt at last they were of one mind and one heart.

He bent to kiss her.

But it was a mistake.

The top half of the dry stone wall moved, and Marie cried out. Bernard seized her arms and thrust his own weight back on his heels with a lurch that jerked Marie up and perpendicular. Half a dozen enormous stones crashed and rolled down from the top of the wall. Marie cried out again as Bernard's rescuing motion pulled her forcibly against him, her face slapping hard against his chest and her lips grazing the fancy clip of his pen. The pen cut her upper lip slightly as her top teeth dug into her lower lip, wounding it inside.

"So sorry." Bernard dabbed her mouth with a handkerchief. "I pulled you too violently."

"It was a good thing you did," Marie said, looking at the debris below her. "I might easily have been down there with some of those stones on top of me."

Bernard held her arms tightly, scrutinizing her face.

"Are you all right otherwise?"

"Fine . . . only . . ." She began to smile.

"Only what?"

"Only I'm quite unkissable now," she said.

Bernard smiled, though he didn't really find it quite so funny.

*How Bernard faced Eve's further advances, and how he
received momentous tidings from Dr. Fisher*

A day or two later, Bernard began to think maybe he shouldn't
live much longer with mother and daughter. It wasn't that Eve
had been anything but cheerful since he'd treated her morning
advances so coolly. Indeed he admired the way she behaved
as though nothing had happened to cause any awkwardness
between them. Falling in love with her daughter, though, made
cool rejection of the mother seem cruel, caddish even.

Then one morning Marie left, saying she'd be out late that
night and not to keep supper for her.

That evening Eve chatted enthusiastically, mostly about
Marie—her past and present. It was almost as though Eve was
aware of Bernard's feelings for Marie and was trying to encourage
them. When they had cleared the table and washed up, Eve said
she was going to have a bath and turn in early.

Bernard settled himself down on the sofa before the fire with
a detective novel found among Eve's books, but it was not very
long before Eve returned, fresh from the bathroom and oozing
with the fragrance of powder and perfume. As she came and
sat down on the sofa at Bernard's side, he sensed a renewal of

the forthcomingness that had brought her to his room on that first morning in the cottage. It was a pity, he thought, that he couldn't find more satisfaction in the situation so changed from that of more than twenty years ago.

She gently lifted his book from his hands. "Bernatd, I want to talk to you."

He didn't move and avoided her gaze. She took his upper arm between her hands.

"Bernard, do you remember that night at Mound Top?"

"Which night?"

He knew very well which night. But he was determined to reject her persistent attempts to make the present contain the past. The new attempt jarred even in advance of her recollections.

"When we drove up there in your father's car. I often think about it, Bernard . . ."

The unfinished sentence trailed away as she raised her hand and gently touched his chin. Bernard remembered clearly enough. They had driven up the long climb past the golf course and the cottages and turned right at the junction with Mound Top Lane. Pushing up the hill beyond the reservoir and past the Old Nag's Head, they had branched to the right again along a little-used lane—a lonely detour right down to Yew's Corner and the Snake's Head. Somewhere, between the sparse farms and barns, they'd pulled into a gateway. The city lights were miles away in the misty basin deep below them. And what was so special about the occasion that Eve should recall it now? He knew, and she guessed that he knew. It was the first time they had sat alone together in a car after dark, taking advantage of the remoteness and the isolation in each other's arms.

82

The memory was vivid enough for Bernard to realize that Eve was curling herself against his left arm now on the sofa of Netherhome Lodge exactly as she had done in the car years ago. Yet there was no emotional pull in the parallel, only embarrassment. What connection had that distant night and those gentle gestures with this overwhelming presence now pressing against him? What connection had that innocent girl of seventeen with this experienced wife of Roger Knight? He could recall from the past an unspoilt delicacy, a simplicity of youthfulness. The memory made this present encounter painfully disparate. He closed his eyes in mute resistance as Eve brought her neck close against his shoulder and spoke in a tone of dreamy reminiscence.

"I've never forgotten it, Bernard. You said some lovely things to me that night."

Bernard writhed inwardly. She surely wasn't going to repeat them . . .

"It was wonderful, Bernard. You read a poem you had written to my . . . to me," she whispered as the perfume of talcum powder rose from the neck and face pressing his shoulder. "I still know it by heart, Bernard, do you?"

"No . . . I mean . . . yes, of course." He was desperate to forestall a verbatim rehearsal.

"I kept a copy right to the end. Sometimes I used to recite it to myself. Especially that lovely verse . . ."

This was more than Bernard could endure. At all costs she must be silenced. Without saying a word, he put his hands to her head, pulled her mouth to his, and kissed her. *At all costs*, he thought. *At all costs.*

83

When the door opened and Marie came in, Bernard began to think that the cost had been too high. It wasn't that he and Eve got too far, but he was, after all, found with the mother in his arms by the daughter he loved.

The daughter just said, "Hello, I'm back," and the words hung for a second or two in the air, awkwardly awaiting an appropriate response.

What could Bernard say, with Eve nestling against him in seemingly amorous entanglement? His lips struggled for a moment to shape a response, but he quickly abandoned the effort. After all, "Ah, so you are!" would sound ridiculous, almost as out of place as "Good evening, and how are you?"

Marie quietly and discreetly went to her room. As if unwilling to help, Eve lifted herself into an upright position at his side only after Marie had left the room. Then, with a degree of self-composure that Bernard found unbearable, she stood up, leaned over, kissed him on the forehead, said good night, and departed.

Bernard began to brood alone about his drab, emotionless performance. To kiss a woman just to keep her quiet was surely a desperate act. Somehow a price would have to be paid for it. How could he make sure that his action tonight wasn't totally misinterpreted? Whatever would be the right way of making clear to Eve how he regarded his own performance? How could he fitly address her tomorrow? *"Any complaints?"* He framed the question mentally, mocking himself and her. *"Satisfied users are asked to bring our services to the notice of their friends."* No, there was no way out to true humor.

He brushed the remaining traces of Eve's powder from his

jacket and wryly congratulated himself on having at least made a response to her demand for affection. *"But your heart was not in what you were doing, Dayman!"* A teacher's rebuke came back from his school days. *"Bernard should demand more of himself. He is adept at going through the motions, but something more than competence is expected of him."*

Bernard decided that it had proved an apt, indeed prophetic, judgment.

Next day Bernard strode down to Hertham, past the cottages and villas, the smart terraces and meaner terraces, and finally onto Market Street. He crossed the road and turned right, retracing the route he'd first followed with Eve. How long ago was that? It seemed ages but in fact was little more than a week ago.

He was driven by a sudden desire to act. The impulse was no doubt the result of suffering a hundred petty, and less petty, frustrations. The most recent one, the unwanted entanglement with Eve, must presumably have disgusted Marie, and it left him floundering, confused. Though he was determined to act, he really had no idea what to do. Part of his frustration lay in the fact that there was nothing he could do. So he decided to go and see the one person he thought he could talk to . . .

Dr. Fisher.

Bernard stared into Godfrey and Son's window, but no face appeared with ritual smile, so he went inside and rang the bell. Dr. Fisher emerged behind the counter and bowed slightly to him. He didn't offer to shake hands. Indeed he held his hands together before his stomach as though involved in some ceremony.

"Let us sit," he said.

"Speaking to you as an agent—" Bernard began.

"You must, for that's what I am."

"I mean, not just as a friend."

"Of course not. Something more than a friend, much more."

"I must apologize if I'm wasting your time."

"My eternity," Dr. Fisher corrected him, "to be precise."

"I've come to see you, yet I haven't really anything to say that's worth listening to."

"We are used to clients."

"I've made rather a mess of things in my first days here."

Dr. Fisher nodded silently.

"I don't seem to have made much progress."

"Progress? Were you expecting that?"

There was an awkward silence. Bernard felt that he was beating about the bush and that Dr. Fisher intended him to feel like that. He took the bull by the horns.

"Naturally, I'd like to go to the New Town."

"Naturally."

"But I haven't a hope."

"Why not?"

"Because of the Waiting List and the selection procedures."

Dr. Fisher sighed. "My dear Bernard, do be rational. How can you say that you are deprived of hope for a place in the New Town by the Waiting List and the selection procedures? That is nonsensical. The Waiting List and the selection procedures exist purely and simply for the purpose of enabling people to get to the New Town. That's what they're for. Surely you do not assert that they impede what they are precisely designed to effect?"

Bernard felt rebuked. "No, I'm not saying that. At least I didn't mean to say that. There's nothing wrong with the selection procedures, I'm sure."

"Sure?"

Bernard furrowed his forehead. "I think so."

"Then what is really wrong?"

Bernard shrugged his shoulders. "Me, I suppose."

"Ah!" A light shone in Dr. Fisher's eyes.

"I'll never get on the List. If Marie isn't on the List after all this time, what hope have I?"

"Marie is all but nominated," Dr. Fisher reminded him.

"She deserves to be."

"She would not be nominated otherwise."

"She doesn't belong here, with the collapsing floors and leaking roofs," Bernard mused.

"She is not discontented here."

"No. That's the funny thing. Marie doesn't complain about the conditions, yet she doesn't fit in either. Now, Eve does complain, yet she's more at home here in many ways."

"You are full of paradoxes this morning, Bernard. Perhaps before you go you will tell me why you've come."

"I've come because I couldn't think of anything better to do."

"A good reason indeed."

"And I simply had to do something."

"You had." Dr. Fisher nodded wisely.

There was silence. Dr. Fisher sat still, as if waiting for something. Bernard fidgeted, and his eyes nervously traced the edges of the surrounding oak panels. Eventually Dr. Fisher prodded him into speech again. "You haven't come to ask to be helped to get on the Waiting List?"

Bernard shook his head.

"Why not?"

"Because it wouldn't be any use."

"Don't you really want to be on the Waiting List?"

"Of course I do."

"Then how do you know it wouldn't be any good to ask for help?"

"I compare myself with Marie. She has struggled for a long time to collect her three references. Now she's got them. If it takes so long for a person of her quality and attractiveness to collect three references, how long is it going to take the likes of me?"

Dr. Fisher nodded thoughtfully. "I see your point." There was gravity in his tone. "Though I'm not in favor, generally speaking, of personal comparisons such as you have just been making between Marie and yourself, I recognize the force of your argument."

Bernard hung his head. "The truth is, I can see no earthly reason why anyone should recommend me for a place."

"No earthly reason," Dr. Fisher repeated. "That's a point."

"No. I'm sure I couldn't find anyone to back me up. Knowing myself as I do, I'm sure it wouldn't be right to ask anyone. I can't remember ever having put anyone under the kind of obligation that would justify me in asking them for a reference. I simply haven't the basis for making a start in the search for references. I couldn't do it."

"This is interesting, Bernard." Dr. Fisher searched his eyes intently. "I believe you are virtually classifying yourself as what we call a 'pauper.'"

"Not a bad description of me in a way." Bernard smiled wryly.

"A 'self-professed friendless pauper' within the meaning of the act," Dr. Fisher muttered meditatively. "Now, let me see, where's Peterstone and Rockcliff?"

He bent down and rummaged about under the counter, then rose again with a black leather volume. "This is our Book of Common Law." He riffled through the pages. "I think you may qualify for special treatment under the Godfrey Bequest. If you do . . . ah yes, here we are. The Godfrey Bequest. Article sixteen, article seventeen, article eighteen. This is the one we want, I think. Clause one, clause two, clause three. This is it, clause four of article eighteen: 'Any applicant freely admitting as a fact (and not lamenting as an injustice) his or her own total lack of referential potential shall be classed as a self-professed friendless pauper, and as such shall be automatically entitled to full referential accreditation in the name of the company.'" Dr. Fisher brightly slapped the book shut. "You're in the clear. Let's fill out your form now." He handed Bernard a copy of the form of application for inclusion on the Waiting List. "Name, address, dates, the usual family particulars, nothing that need worry you. You'd better have one of these leaflets too. Put this in your pocket."

Bernard was bewildered, but Dr. Fisher's determination and urgency carried him along. He took the folded leaflet, noted only the words "Godfrey and Son" on the front, and put it in his pocket. Then he took out his pen and began to fill in the form.

"It's a wonderful thing, the Godfrey Bequest, a wonderful thing," Dr. Fisher said, then started to hum as Bernard wrote. He reached down under the desk and took into his hands some rubber stamps and a stamp pad.

Meanwhile, Bernard completed the form, except for three awesome spaces at the bottom, where the rubric read: "Reference No. 1: Accepted/Rejected. Reference No. 2: Accepted/Rejected. Reference No. 3: Accepted/Rejected." He had studied these lines before. The empty spaces seemed to be the most formidable things he had set eyes on in his sojourn at Old Hertham.

Dr. Fisher picked up his rubber stamps one by one. He flourished and pressed each one in turn. Then he said, "Signed and sealed. Alph Godfrey, Christopher Godfrey, and Henry G. Host, company secretary. Your form of application is now complete. You owe your thanks to the Godfrey Bequest."

"I don't understand." Bernard blinked uncomprehendingly. "It seems rather improper."

"Not in the least. As patron of our firm, Sir Alph Godfrey had every right to do what he wanted with it. In fact, he put the whole business in the hands of his son, Christopher Godfrey, while he himself concentrated on laying the foundations of the New Town. That's ancient history, of course. People have always argued about it, and some have thought that Sir Alph ought to have kept his hands on everything himself. Well, it's true that Godfrey Jr. was a bit of an eccentric. He kept odd company, you know, and got himself a name for it. People were fussier in those days than they are now, and he let himself in for a lot of criticism. They said young Christopher was not the person his father was. They thought him not quite respectable, seemingly more interested in helping lame dogs and drinking with down-and-outs than in running the firm smoothly. Then again others will tell you that even as a boy Christopher was really quite precociously keen on his father's business. Anyway, Christopher left this extraordinary will behind him when he moved officially to the New Town himself. In its general outline, the will is a straightforward list of benefactions, but the detailed clauses are full of surprises when you get the legal men to expound them."

Dr. Fisher tapped his black Book of Common Law. "Peterstone and Rockcliff did a wonderful job of explanation and analysis here. So as far as you are concerned, there can be no argument. The terms of the will are absolutely clear. Technically, you're a pauper, a self-professed friendless pauper. And a pauper of that kind has the right to unconditional references in the company's own name. You are now entitled to an immediate public hearing. Once that is out of the way, your name goes slap onto the Waiting List."

"Is this quite fair?" Bernard asked. "I mean, couldn't anyone come here and make the same claim?"

Dr. Fisher looked around for a moment as though asking himself whether it would be proper to answer this question. Then he stood up and unhooked the memorandum pad (the one that looked like a calendar) from the wall behind him.

"You see that?"

He pointed to a little circular hole in the wall. It had not actually been covered by the pad, but it was so close to the bottom edge of the cardboard that, because of the way the light fell from the window to Dr. Fisher's right, it had in fact been so shadowed as to be unnoticeable.

"There's a very sensitive microscopic lens through there, focused on the chair where you're now sitting, and the camera is linked to a lie detector. The lie detector registers its findings down here." The doctor pointed under the counter. "There's a little orange bulb that flashes on and off. You couldn't possibly see it from your side of the counter."

Bernard was intrigued by the incongruity between the archaic atmosphere of the agency's office, with its polished oak and huge leather-bound volumes, and the modern devices that these very furnishings concealed. How could it be that Dr. Fisher himself exuded a mixture of old-world courtesy and learnedness yet dwelled in a world of push buttons and flashbulbs? Bernard was beginning to picture the unseen depths behind the counter from which the venerable old volumes had been extracted as something like an airliner's control panel. He stared hard at Dr. Fisher.

"I puzzle you, Bernard, and amuse you too. Why?"

"This old-fashioned office with its elaborate machinery . . ." Bernard stumbled to explain. "The . . . contrast between the two . . ."

"I know of no equation between the traditional and the inefficient, and still less between the old-fashioned and the ingenuous. If someone chooses to be taken in by the age of our firm and our taste for the traditional in office furnishings and to assume that we're therefore gullible amateurs in our trade, then so much the worse for them." Dr. Fisher's smile remained as tranquil and good-humored as ever, but there was a sharpness in his voice, an air of finality to what he said.

Bernard quickly turned the subject back to his own position. "What's the next step, Dr. Fisher?"

"To wait."

"I don't have to do anything?"

"The next step is ours. You have put yourself into our hands as a pauper. We shall arrange for your hearing. You will be informed of the time and place in due course."

How news of Bernard's good fortune was received at Netherhome Lodge, and how Len lost his footing in Hertham

With mixed feelings Bernard walked back to the cottage. He felt glad that he'd achieved something, but it was a gladness he'd rather have shared. Indeed it had to be shared—with Marie. But a dark cloud now hung over his relationship with her, the memory of her unexpected return home last night.

Those simple words, *"Hello, I'm back,"* stuck in his mind now as uncomfortably as they'd stuck in the distance between them when she'd entered the room.

How could he hope to explain? If he were chivalrous enough to claim all responsibility for the affair, he would lower himself in Marie's eyes in one way. If he blamed everything on Eve's crude initiatives, he might well lower himself in her eyes even more in another way.

Underneath his apprehension ran a curious thread of hope. A state of misunderstanding with Marie was somehow unthinkable. By temperament she had a vested interest in clarity. Surely the news he brought from Godfreys' would unite the two of them in a common search for a new home.

Brooding on the curious developments of the last hour or so, he suddenly realized he'd never read the folded leaflet Dr. Fisher had handed him when the application form was suddenly stamped. Bernard pulled the brochure from his pocket and studied it as he walked.

GODFREY AND SON

ESTATE AGENTS

MARKET STREET—OLD HERTHAM

Godfrey and Son is an old, established firm dealing in real estate and specializing in properties in the New Town. All our officers are officially accredited agents working on a commission basis. Each of them has qualified as an Associate of the Guaranteed Accommodation Provision Establishment (AGAPE). We draw attention to the fact that, as the law now stands, no duty-free contracts or open-ended agreements can be entered into. Clients are warned against the activities of unauthorized mushroom firms styling themselves "agencies" and offering to provide the usual services on a duty-free basis.

Advice to Newcomers

1. Be aware that a number of houses in New Town can be made immediately available in exchange for the surrender of whole life policies previously taken out by clients under the special conditions and provisions of the Christopher Godfrey Endowment Assurance Scheme. (This applies only where premiums have been fully and regularly paid up over an extended period.)
2. If you have been a regular subscriber to a recognized

friendly society and have accumulated bonds under the Incorporated Family Protection Trust or have substantial deposits in any nonprofit charitable institution, consult one of our agents about converting holdings. Expert advice is given about the current value of any assets to be realized.

3. Shareholders who have a record of lifelong investment in the Future Accommodation Insurance Trust— Hertham (FAITH) will be granted benefits proportionate to their respective holdings.

4. If you had the foresight to make regular use in the past of contacts provided by the Council of Hertham's Upmarket Residence Customer Hotline (CHURCH), draw an agent's attention to your record.

5. Newcomers who during their lifetimes failed to take the precaution of insuring in any way against the possibility of future loss of habitation should enquire about the special provisions on offer through the Christopher Godfrey Bequest. Under its terms numerous benefits are available for needy applicants.

GODFREY AND SON FOR NEW TOWN HOMES ON ROCK-BOTTOM TERMS

For further assistance at any time, call the Christopher Godfrey Helpline:
Freephone NT 13579246810

The more Bernard read of Godfrey and Son's publicity material, the less sure was he that effective communication took place between Dr. Fisher and himself. But at least the agent's words about the Waiting List had been clear enough, and it appeared he was benefiting under the provisions made in clause five for totally uninsured newcomers. It would be good to go over all this with Marie.

With that in mind, Bernard was acutely disappointed to find, when he got back to the cottage, that Len was a guest at supper. Presumably, Eve had taken pity on him after the loss of his car. And indeed tonight the man was full of complaints against the authorities—against what he called the "official vandalism" of neglecting Old Hertham's housing. The evening meal was punctuated by his various outbursts. Afterward an awkward silence prevailed, broken eventually by a seemingly challenging inquiry from Eve.

"You haven't told us what you've been doing all day, Bernard."

Bernard didn't reply immediately. He was less than anxious to talk of what was on his mind.

"Nothing special?" Eve pressed as to suggest he was hiding something.

"Only an interview at Godfreys'," Bernard said quietly, casually, believing Eve wouldn't want to pursue the topic.

"The agents?" Len asked with ominous emphasis.

"Yes."

"They're racketeers. They'll do you no good."

"They seem prepared to help customers." Bernard put the case as vaguely as he could.

"The Godfreys are the biggest sharks in the market. Their whole record is against them. Everyone knows that they were founded on a very dubious basis. Old Alph Godfrey was a mystery man. By all accounts nobody in Hertham ever saw him."

"Some people claimed to have seen him," Marie said.

"They certainly did. But I don't know of any reputable historical scholar who would take their claims seriously today. As for his son, Christopher, his career speaks for itself. He was a complete failure as a director, and the firm had to be propped up by shareholders after he absconded to the New Town to join his father. If the shareholders hadn't rallied, the firm would have gone bust. Young Godfrey fleeced the firm of capital assets to finance his pet schemes. They were supposed to be philanthropic, but they were never properly financed, and they did precious little good to anyone. Take that Feed the Hungry Fund he set up. It was starved of money. The endowment was supposed to supply a free fish-and-chip dinner once a year to five thousand hungry people, but when it came to the point, the total annual interest was scarcely enough to buy five packets of potato chips and three little herrings.

"And what about that Wine for Weddings Endowment Fund? The whole idea was crazy. The parents of brides were urged to go to one of the agents with a few bottles of water and the agents would swap them for bottles of wine. The stuff the parents were given was so strong that when the toasts came along and the glasses were emptied, no one could stand up. Everybody fell about the room. The trouble was that the board of directors Godfrey Jr. gathered around himself were a bunch of incompetents. I expect they'd been told to find a knockout vintage and had taken the words too literally. None of them had any business experience or financial expertise except for that fellow Chariot, or whatever he was called. And he worried about it so much that he had a breakdown and put his head in the gas oven. The rest of them were like Christopher himself, a bunch of amateurs, two or three of them just picked up at the dockside."

Bernard felt no longer able to see his benefactors so crudely written off. "Well," he said quietly, "The Godfreys have been kind to me."

"Have they? And in what way?"

Reticence was no longer an option. "They've helped me to a hearing."

"A hearing!" Eve shrieked. "Already! You haven't been here five minutes. What about references?"

"They've given me some themselves."

"Just like that?"

"Yes, just like that, strange as it is. Formal references of their own under the terms of some special bequest."

"They're not worth the paper they're written on," Len cut in. "Everyone knows the Godfrey Bequest is nothing but an advertising gimmick."

"Do they?" Marie queried. "Christopher Godfrey certainly left a remarkable will."

"It was bogus. False."

"That's your opinion."

"It was mostly concocted by his accomplices after he'd gone off to the New Town. They wanted to make it appear that he hadn't left everyone in the lurch. They thought they ought to sharpen his image. There were at least four supposedly official biographies, but they were full of discrepancies. They didn't

100

seem to know whether to advertise him as a New Age guru with a taste for opting out of the rat race or as a quack practitioner of alternative medicine. He was reputed to have cured a few people whose doctors had written them off. It seems that he dabbled in organic homeopathic treatments, and they claimed that he brought remissions to people with all manner of ailments. They called it 'Christopher Godfrey's holistic approach.' The most exaggerated claims were made for it. There was an absurd pretense that young Godfrey had only to tell someone to get out of his wheelchair and the fellow would find that he could jump up and push it home.

"They tried to build him up as a miracle-monger. They said he had only to stand up and put his hand in the air and the stormy Atlantic would turn itself into a smooth duck pond. But when a poor farmer begged him to cure his stock of swine fever, it proved disastrous. Godfrey just said, 'Abracadabra,' and the entire herd of pigs went mad and jumped off a cliff into the sea.

"He was a real menace politically too. He seems to have been a Marxist or something, to judge from the things he said about plutocrats and bureaucrats. There were plenty of question marks on the moral side, as well. Some of his best friends were notorious women. At least one had been a call girl before she joined his circle. She was a bit crazy too. They were sitting together after dinner one evening when she suddenly poured a whole bottle of Chanel over his head. Just like that."

Sitting there near Marie, whom he would dearly have liked to talk to, Bernard wished only that the man would shut up, but ironically it was Eve who came to the rescue.

"You'll excuse us, Bernard, won't you? Len and I have some

101

Trust business to go into, and we don't want to bore you with it."

So Eve was to take Len out of the room. Nothing could have suited Bernard more. He looked across at Marie, sitting opposite him, staring at the fire; she showed no inclination to move. Eve smiled graciously at them as she left.

"We shouldn't be long," she said.

To Bernard's surprise, Marie broke the ice as soon as they were left alone. "I was very excited to hear your good news, Bernard. Tell me all about it."

Bernard gave her a full account of his interview with Dr. Fisher.

"So it was very simple in the end," Marie said. "These things always are."

"If you happen to be a pauper . . ."

"A genuine self-professed one. You scored a point there—" Marie interrupted herself. "What was that?"

The two of them stared hard at each other.

"Did you feel it?" Marie asked. "A sort of vibration?"

Bernard nodded. They waited, silent, eyes searching the corners of the room and running along the carpet. After some seconds they relaxed.

"I thought it was underneath us," Bernard said.

"I thought it was going to be. That's what it felt like to me, something that was going to happen and didn't."

"Subsidence?"

"I suppose we've got it on the brain. That's what happens once you've had a taste of it. You keep casting your eyes on the walls and the floors."

"It ought to work the other way around," Bernard said. "I've just been in the middle of a case of subsidence myself, and surely these cases can't be all that common. Statistically speaking, my chances of a subsidence-free stretch now must be very high, and my chances of a second dose almost nil. The law of averages does count for something. I think an insurance company would back me on this one."

"You're as persuasive as an advocate for one of those betting systems, and I wouldn't put my money on any of them."

"You're not the betting type, Marie. You're too reasonable." He leaned forward toward her. "And that's why I think perhaps, though I don't deserve it, you might let me explain about last night."

"Last night?" The questioning tone was genuine.

"Last night when you came home."

"Of course." She spoke without emotion, and there was a kind of half smile about her mouth and a stillness about her eyes that seemed to convey some such message as *Need we bother?*

Bernard stared at her, rather bewildered. Did it not matter to her? Had she not been worried by what she had seen? If so, then she certainly was not as involved with him as he was with her. Otherwise she couldn't be so calm. Surely it would be better for his prospects if she showed some . . . some what? Jealousy? Anxiety? Disappointment? Whatever it was, the brown eyes and the calm voice were free of it.

They heard footsteps in the passage outside. They heard the front door open.

"Len is going," Marie said, "without even coming in to say good night."

"We're not his best friends obviously!"

Three—or was it four or five or six?—astonishing things happened with lightning rapidity. There seemed to be a near-simultaneous multiple concentration of catastrophic shocks; the lights in the cottage went out, Len shouted from the doorway, and something collapsed with a thud. A car, two cars at least, roared up to the cottage, police sirens wailing. The glare from their headlights and roof searchlights flooded through the curtains into the now dark room.

The sirens wailed out, and a voice thundered through the powerful amplifiers: "Stay where you are. Stay where you are. Stay where you are, Netherhome Lodge. Stay where you are, Hillside. Stay where you are until advised. Subsidence outside. Stay where you are."

Marie jumped up and made for the door, Bernard following. The blaze of lights from the road below flooded the garden, and police were scrambling up through the bushes to the cottage. They held torches and sticks and prodded the ground ahead of them. A fissure had opened up in the earth, running for as far as Bernard could see in the darkness. It was exactly parallel with the front wall of the cottage. There was little more than a yard between the cottage wall and the edge of the gigantic crack. A tributary crack, at right angles to the main one, ran up the cottage garden to the Italian summerhouse and Bernard's bedroom. The once delightful building had collapsed and was now a heap of rubble, half lost down the crack.

Shaking his head, a policeman came face-to-face with Bernard, but at a distance of some yards, across the black pit. "It's a bad case of subsidence. More like an earth tremor, judging from the shape of the thing."

Eve rushed back to the door.

"Is he all right? Len?"

"Someone missing, lady?"

"My friend Len. He was just leaving when it happened." She gasped and looked into the rubble. "Could he have fallen in?"

The policeman turned his powerful torch into the hole; the light was lost in the black depths. He shook his head.

"I should take the lady in, sir," he said to Bernard.

Marie led her weeping mother back into the sitting room.

"What about the house, officer?" Bernard put his question gently.

"I don't think there's any immediate danger. Not just now. It's a miracle that the crack just missed you. You've lost your outbuilding, I'm afraid."

From what he could see in the glare of the lights, it appeared to Bernard that the crack had missed the road except for a small gash at the side, about five feet long but not more than eighteen inches wide and very shallow. That hole had already been covered with an iron plate of the standard type that Bernard now recognized as being designed for this purpose. He had already seen enough of them to realize that the Council Engineer's Department must keep an enormous stock of these plates in various sizes.

Outside Netherhome Lodge itself, there was a busy scene. The two police cars had become three, and there was a green van from the Council Engineer's Department, plus a vehicle Bernard would have called a fire truck had he not known that it belonged to the Council Subsidence Brigade.

Considering all the circumstances, Bernard found it a strangely unmoving scene. The drama of the unexpected disaster wasn't what struck him most. Rather, it was the efficiency of the machinery that was coping with it. The officers went about their business briskly, and it wasn't long before a policeman came back to report to Bernard, and Marie joined him at the door.

"You can safely stay in the house, sir," the officer reported. "No immediate danger. The engineers will be around tomorrow to shore up the front wall and make some sort of temporary bridge over the crevice. You're very lucky people." The policeman sounded grand, as though he had had a part in granting the good fortune.

"I can't see it," Bernard said.

"Why, your house is on a bit of ground that hasn't budged an inch. There must be a wedge of good tough rock underneath it. If the place had been built a few yards this way, you'd have had the walls in the road and the roof on your heads. Or you might have been lost down there." He pointed to the fissure.

"What about Len?" Marie asked. "Have they got him out?"

"No sign of him, but they've got rope ladders down, and the brigade is making a thorough search. The trouble is that they don't know how deep it goes. They haven't found the bottom yet."

"It doesn't sound so good," Bernard said, sure that they ought to be prepared for the worst.

"Not at all good," the policeman agreed.

"Len has had bad luck," Bernard told him. "He lost his car down a hole a day or two ago."

"Ah!" The policeman nodded gravely. "It's the way things happen sometimes. I've known a dog to go down one week and its master to follow it the next."

"Bernard," Marie said, taking his arm, "you'll have to take over my bedroom. I'll move into the storage room next to Mother. It's big enough for me, and I've slept there before."

How Netherhome Lodge was buttressed, and how news was received there of Marie's hearing

Men came the next day from the Council Engineer's Department and propped up the front of the cottage with great wooden buttresses.

"They're probably not necessary," the foreman told Bernard, "but you never know."

Bernard thought it ironic that they found it advisable to wedge the buttresses against the side of the rift that had created the need for them.

"We might as well make use of it now that it's there," the foreman said.

His workmen set about constructing a bridge over the fissure in the garden. Wooden beams were covered with the standard iron plates and bolted into place, and more wooden buttresses were wedged against the sides of the rift. Bernard wondered whether this wasn't an ominous arrangement. The rift's full depths were unexplored, and Len was lost in them.

The foreman was prepared to be philosophical about this loss and the mystery surrounding it. "We don't know how deep the rift is," he said. "We don't know whether it opens up into one of the exploratory shafts dug when there was an attempt to map the system or whether the earth has been cut right down to one of the old horizontal workings." He sighed. "I don't think we'll know. It would be too expensive to get all the gear over here that would be needed to make a full search. And this is a terrible site to work on, sir. What could we do, jammed between the rift and the road on a bit of sloping garden?"

"And Len?" Bernard queried.

"We do lose people from time to time."

"Surely no expense should be spared when a man's safety is at stake?"

"No expense?" The foreman shook his head. "I think you'll find the assessor's report will be against any further operations here."

Inside the cottage Bernard had to face an emotional Eve. He found her stiffly upright on a chair in the sitting room, her pose anything but relaxed. The atmosphere was thick with the tension expressed in the formal posture, the folded arms, and the fixed stare.

"Marie has deceived me," she said gravely.

"Oh, surely not, Eve."

"Look at that."

She handed him the week's edition of the *Hertham Gazette*, folded so that he could find the right place. He stared at the middle page, a page seemingly given over to New Town news and gossip. Eve pointed to the columns he was meant to read:

THE WAITING LIST

RECENT ADDITIONS

At this week's hearings at Hertham Town Hall, several candidates were successful in satisfying the bench of their just claim to inclusion on the Waiting List. In many cases claims were sustained against objections from the public gallery, and our correspondent reports on the week in the court as a fairly lively one, involving numerous heated exchanges. (Summaries of some of the more interesting legal wrangles will be found on page 7.) Among the successful candidates, listed below, names marked with an asterisk (*) achieved the honor of unopposed nomination to the Waiting List.

Standing out from a list of some twenty or so names were four or five asterisked ones, including "Marie Knight*, Netherhome Lodge."

Bernard couldn't pretend to share Eve's shock at this piece of news. In one respect he was delighted. Seeing himself on the brink of a hearing, he was most anxious that his progress should run in parallel with Marie's. Nevertheless, it niggled him that Marie hadn't mentioned the hearing to him. Was she less keen to share intimacies with him than he'd been with her? Or was it that she didn't want him to feel she was leaving him behind?

He studied the news item again. Lower down the column, he read "Unsuccessful candidates. See next column." In that next column ran a list of deferred candidates almost half as long as the list of successful candidates. The wording was not heartening:

The following candidates were unable fully to sustain their claims on the spot against objections raised from the public gallery. The cases were recorded as meriting further examination. The bench therefore ruled that the candidates' applications must be held in

111

abeyance with the right of further hearings upon completion of the necessary formalities.

Under this notice, with its block of about half a dozen names, there was a more dismal paragraph still:

The following candidates were totally unable to sustain their claims against objections raised from the public gallery. Objections were upheld. The bench therefore ruled the applications null and void.

The sight of the sad handful of names, compared with the twenty or so successful candidates, was saddening. Quick to give such comparisons an arithmetical form, Bernard reckoned that the weighting of chances for a successful hearing was only about one in three. He'd assumed that a hearing was little more than a formality.

Eve sensed his dismay but misread it. "I'm not surprised that you're shocked, Bernard. It hurt me deeply. Marie never breathed a word about this."

Bernard had to make an effort to find the right things to say. "She didn't want to hurt you . . . I don't think she's to be blamed."

He was relieved to find that Eve's emotions were involved with Marie and not him. Since the uncomfortable conclusion of their seemingly passionate embrace on the sofa, he had feared that Eve might assume a more possessive role toward him, a role that presupposed an intimate understanding between them. But Eve had behaved toward him as though the incident had never occurred. *Like mother like daughter in that respect*, he said to himself.

As Eve dabbed her eyes with her handkerchief, Bernard sat

down and waited in silence. The *Hertham Gazette* still lay open in his hands. His eye was caught by an advertisement inserted strategically under the various items about the hearings:

GODFREY & SON—AMDG

The Applications Management Director at Godfreys' (AMDG) wishes to tender the company's warmest congratulations to all who have been successful in this week's hearings and will be happy to advise applicants who have been disappointed in this respect.

> For further assistance at any time, call the Christopher Godfrey Helpline:
> Freephone NT 13579246810

It appeared that Dr. Fisher kept his eyes on the ball, but as Bernard turned the page of the newspaper, a rather different item came into view:

DEMO BY ASB

A small group of protesters gathered outside the town hall doors on Tuesday, holding placards that read STOP THIS FARCE. Their spokesperson said they were members of the Anti-selection Brigade who believed that hearings should be abolished. "We are against all such playacting. As NT houses become available, they should be allotted to applicants in alphabetical order, and applicants informed by phone or by email."

Bernard thought he must now have stumbled on the section of the newspaper devoted to opposition groups, for the following item appeared underneath:

The Regional Clearance Policy was subjected to withering scorn at this week's meeting of the Old Hertham Preservation Trust. The guest speaker, Professor Simpkins, well-known for his controversial views, lambasted the estate agencies and called for a campaign to resist their influence.

Bernard might have read more, but Eve's renewed sobbing interrupted him.

"She'll leave us," she began. "She'll go off on her own. She deserves what's coming to her."

"It looks as though she's going to get what we all want, what we all want deep down. Isn't that true, Eve?"

"She's getting it without any thought of us. She's happy to go her own way and leave me behind."

"Then you don't want to be left behind, Eve?" Bernard hoped he was seeing a positive opening at last.

"I wouldn't leave here for anything. I wouldn't have a new house thrown at me. Vulgar things, full of kitchen fittings and those horrible heating vents. They even have air-conditioning. Think of it. Windows that won't open . . ."

"Better than windows that won't shut," Bernard muttered.

"Netherhome Lodge is my home. I love every inch of it."

"But it's disintegrating."

"To me it's beautiful."

"It was once, no doubt. But not now, surrounded by pit props and patched with roofing felt."

"It's still beautiful, a beautiful house in a beautiful garden."

Bernard became exasperated. "See things as they are, Eve. Your beautiful garden has a fenced-off pit that makes it look like a cross between a hen run and a tipping site. The path is plastered with cast-iron plates that look like the throwouts from railway sheds shut down at the end of the age of steam."

Bernard's scorn was withering. It was meant to shake Eve free of her dream picture of Netherhome Lodge, but Bernard saw it failing in her hardened eyes and knew he had struck the wrong note.

"I'm sorry, Eve. I shouldn't have put it like that. There's plenty of homeliness here. But I can understand how Marie wants to get away from the frustrations we all have to put up with here. Whatever you feel about Netherhome Lodge, you have to remember that it's in a clearance area. In the long run, it's done for. You and I know that."

"It needn't be done for. If only people would actually do something about it instead of fighting for places on the Waiting List, queuing up to get away from their responsibilities. We needn't allow homes to decay. That's why I joined the Preservation Trust. Because it's really trying to do something for people here and now. It's not like your agencies, which seem to think nothing matters except putting people's names down on lists. As if that were any use to them! People want to be helped. They want their homes to be looked after. They don't want to spend all their time filling in forms and badgering other people for references. They won't listen to estate agents who can't share their personal interests and sympathize with them in their difficulties. The Preservation Trust officers do care. They believe in people; they treat them with compassion. Professor Simpkins hit the nail on the head. It isn't good enough to tantalize people with dreams of new houses in the distant future in some place they don't know and that sounds too good to be true anyway. From what they say about it, life in the New Town must be just too perfect to be endured. I'd be utterly bored. Who wants to live in a place where everything works perfectly?"

"It's better than a clearance area where everything breaks down."

"That's what the agents tell you. You're like Marie; you soak in everything they say. I'm sick of them. They don't understand people. They don't know how to relate and communicate. They should take people as they find them. They should start with them where they are. They should learn to be compassionate."

Bernard sighed deeply. Then, determined to get more fully to grips with Eve's train of thought, he leaned forward, taking the arms of his chair in his hands. In doing so, he accidentally pushed his chair back a few inches. Unfortunately, this brought a back leg exactly onto the one area of patched floorboard that could not stand a special pressure because of the lack of a beam underneath it. The deficiency turned the floorboard into a potential seesaw.

Seeing his forward movement, and disliking the prospect of further argument, Eve spoke petulantly. "But for goodness' sake, let's drop it. That's quite enough."

Flinging up his hands in frustration, Bernard threw himself despairingly back once more into the depths of his chair. The sudden shock was too much for the floorboard underneath. It converted itself at once into a seesaw and dropped some inches at the crucial end. Bernard's chair tilted with a jerk and spilled him onto the floor.

How Bernard was given a hearing in the town hall, and how he conducted himself

A brief formal note summoned Bernard to his hearing at Hertham Town Hall. Registered as a friendless pauper and appearing before the court under the protection of the Godfrey Trust, he had been granted free legal aid. The solicitors supplying the aid were named on the note as "Messrs. Raphael, Warden, and Company," but Bernard knew nothing about them and wondered how on earth they could know anything about him.

This question was answered the day of the hearing itself, when Bernard was greeted in the ornate arched corridor of the town hall by an angular figure in a wig and gown.

"Mr. Dayman, I'm Michael Warden of Raphael, Warden, and Company. I represent you."

"Glad to meet you," Bernard said politely, extending his hand to be shaken.

"Oh, quite."

Warden seemed taken aback. What had he been expecting Bernard to say?

"I suppose you want to ask me a lot of questions?" Bernard tried to sound cooperative.

"Not at all."

"But you are representing me, you say?"

"I shall provide such representation as may be needed. We have every hope that little will be required. Of course, you never know. Sometimes, when you least expect it, the objectors rise in their dozens. That's the fun of this work, Bernard. You never know whether you're in for a day of subsidized inertia or of hectic professional extemporization. Speaking personally, I prefer the latter. But I don't expect my clients to share my preference." Warden laughed.

The word *extemporization* troubled Bernard. "You must have some brief to work on, Mr. Warden."

"Don't you worry about that. Godfrey and Son is the best possible company to work for. They give clear instructions and then leave you with a free hand over how you carry them out. They put your case into my hands, and Dr. Fisher supplied a very full dossier on your background and career. I spent last night on it, burning the midnight oil, so I'm well prepared. Though, between you and me, Bernard, I must say, one or two things . . . one or two things . . . I'm not a squeamish person, but dear me. I think you know what I'm getting at."

"You think I might find myself in difficulties?"

"Let's be frank, Bernard. There are episodes here and there, floating about in the dim past. Perhaps they are best forgotten. Who knows? But should a mean-minded person have dug them out and choose to give them a public airing, then we might have to use just that extra bit of ingenuity to keep you in the clear."

"In short, you think I might be snookered," Bernard said.

"That's not the word I should have chosen. But it's apt."

Inside the courtroom, antique wooden benches and enclosures gave the place an air of venerable discomfort. Bernard sat in what looked like an eighteenth-century church pew, with a communicating doorway separating him from Warden in an adjacent pew. Placed as he was, Bernard felt like a criminal on trial before the proceedings even opened. And yet he felt more reassured by the informal conduct of some of the people present.

An official in a wig and a gown vaulted from the door, over all the benches, desks, and partitions in between, to his place below the judge's throne at the center of things. The official's gown floated in the air like wings behind him as he made for his desk in as direct a line as possible.

"That's Gabriel Crowe, the clerk to the court," Warden explained to Bernard. "He believes in going straight to the point."

The hammering of wood against wood produced a sudden hush.

A voice proclaiming, "Be upstanding for His Honor Judge Powers," brought people in the courtroom to their feet.

"He's one of the top rank of the judiciary," Warden whispered.

The judge entered, followed by two other gowned and be-wigged officials, who then sat on either side of him. The judge gave a signal to the clerk, and proceedings opened.

For a tedious few minutes the clerk recited the contents of a formal document in a singsong voice. It was full of legal jargon—"whereas" and "hereunder" and "therein" and "heretofore"—with prolixities that made even the judge yawn.

Bernard waded through the jargon to the essence of it all: the court was informed that he sought to be enrolled on the Waiting

List as an accredited applicant for a house in the New Town, and the people who took a poor view of his fitness should let the court know exactly what they thought of him. This was pressed upon them as their public duty, though they must bear in mind the need to substantiate objections with clear, factual testimony. Bernard shifted his weight. What it all amounted to was that anyone who wanted to block his hopes must now speak or else forever hold their peace.

When the clerk sat down, a sudden change came over the court. Everyone fell silent. Everyone kept dead still. This was the moment of suspense, the moment they were all waiting for . . .

A movement in the public gallery.

A man rose to his feet. "Objection, my lord."

Bernard sought in vain for a glimpse of the familiar in the man's voice, face, or bearing.

"Let us hear," the judge said.

The man waved a piece of paper. "Written evidence, my lord."

The paper was handed down the gallery and across the benches to the clerk of the court, who read it aloud: "Bernard Dayman is not a fit person to be enrolled on the Waiting List, for his claim to desire a New Town house is false. Since he came to Hertham he has never, so far as is known, studied or even read any of the admirable brochures that give descriptions of New Town residences. Nor has he consulted any of the excellent guides to life in New Town—guides that are available everywhere for sale or in libraries. It may be that a claimant can be excused for not looking at any of the Old Town histories, though they trace the events that made construction of the New Town inevitable, but no claimant can be excused for failing to acquire or open a single book or journal on the establishment of New Town, its housing, architecture, planning, or furnishing—or its social life or cultural amenities. So on these grounds we submit that the claimant has not shown such interest in the New Town as to deserve a place on the Waiting List alongside men and women who have for long used their best endeavors to acquaint themselves with New Town and the exciting prospects it offers. We further submit that the claimant is not so much interested in New Town as bored with Hertham."

The judge looked gravely at the paper handed up to him from the clerk.

Warden frowned and whispered to Bernard, "This is a nasty one to deal with. The objectors know what they're doing."

"Whom do you represent?" the judge asked the man in the gallery.

"FOWL, my lord." In a whisper to Bernard while rummaging in his briefcase, Warden explained, "Friends of the Waiting List. They have spies everywhere."

In a moment of quiet, the press reporters in the center of the court bit their pens expectantly.

"The short summary of your case," the judge said, addressing the man in the gallery, "is contained in your last sentence."

"That is so, my lord. We submit that the claimant is not so much interested in the New Town as bored with Hertham."

"Counsel for the claimant," the judge said.

"My lord." Warden rose to his feet respectfully.

"The charge requires an answer."

"Yes, my lord. May I put my client in the box?"

"Of course."

Bernard was approached by a man whose uniform consisted simply of a black, velvet-edged gown over his everyday suit—an outfit easily distinguishable from the legal dignitaries in the room with their striped trousers, white collar tabs, and wigs. The gowned man nodded for Bernard to rise from his pew, then escorted him to a more central site—a sort of witness box in which the occupant stood face-to-face with the judge.

Yet, unlike a witness box, this dock gave the judge the clearest possible view of its occupant while preventing most of the rest of the court from seeing him at all. High sides and a high back blocked the view to the right and to the left, leaving Bernard with a sort of horse's-eye view, a horse freshly equipped with blinders. Compelled to stare at the judge, Bernard felt cornered. If the judge's ornate seat, with its high, carved back and miniature turrets, was as grand as a bishop's throne, his own dismally obscured perch was as furtive as a confessional box. Bernard couldn't even see his own counsel. Was this an intentional limitation?

Warden's voice came floating on the air from nowhere. "My lord, the charge is that my client is not so much interested in the New Town as bored with Hertham. I submit that a charge expressed as a comparison—not so much this as that—is neither legally nor logically valid. I submit, my lord, that if I were to complain of a faithful and attentive husband that he was not so much in love with his wife as uninterested in any potential mistress, you would quite properly urge me to get rid of the comparison, to break up the complaint into its component parts, and to address myself like a rational person to the two questions: Is this man in love with his wife? Is this man interested in other women? Assuming that the court has followed the logic of my argument so far, I beg leave to reduce the ill-expressed and confused accusation to its two basic elements. Is my client interested in the New Town? Is my client bored with Hertham?

"First, is he interested in the New Town? Bernard Dayman, how long had you been here with us in Old Hertham when you first called upon an estate agent? Was it months, weeks, days, hours?"

The judge stared hard at Bernard's eyes.

"About ten minutes, I think."

"And what was the subject of your first interview with the agent?"

"New Town properties and how to obtain one."

"Thank you. My lord, I submit that my client is a person so interested in residence in the New Town that his first action on arriving here was to call upon an agent and inquire about New Town properties. I turn to the second element in the charge. Bernard Dayman, how much had you seen of Hertham when you paid this first visit to the estate agent?"

"A few yards of Market Street and a few shop windows."

"How, in fact, was most of your brief ten minutes here spent before you actually entered the agent's office?"

"Looking in the agent's window."

"Thank you. I submit, my lord, that it is impossible for a man to be driven from Hertham by boredom with the place after only ten minutes' residence here, most of which was occupied in looking in an estate agent's window. Boredom with Hertham was not the motive behind my client's original interest in the New Town. The case against him collapses.

"Lest, however, the court should be swayed by the claimant's alleged lack of interest in the New Town as evidenced by his failure to immerse himself in New Town literature, let me draw the court's attention to the fact that this allegation, even if proved (and I'm not saying that it could be proved), would constitute negative evidence only. Courts cannot be concerned with what people have not done and might have done, but only with what they have done. Negative evidence, as everyone knows, though interesting in corroboration of positive evidence, is in itself inadmissible for the purpose of establishing a case. In this instance we've already demolished the positive case that negative evidence might have been used to corroborate. The evidence is therefore inadmissible.

"Perhaps I may clarify this point by analogy. Suppose I wished to prove that a man was not in love with his wife. To establish that he never took photographs of her would be negative evidence. Such evidence might be of some value in corroborating positive evidence, such as that he criticized his wife's appearance and that he was in the habit of taking photographs of other women. But in itself, in its pure negativity, it would be valueless testimony, inadmissible as the basis of a case. Thank you, my lord."

The judge turned to his fellow magistrates, first on one side, then on the other, exchanging nods.

"Objection answered," he said.

The gowned officer came to lead Bernard back from the box to his pew.

"The man's a wizard," he heard one of the pressmen whisper as he passed them. And indeed Warden's performance struck Bernard as a masterly one. What was so remarkable about it was the slightness of the burden it placed upon the person in the box. He himself had not been asked to explain anything or exemplify anything by going into reasons or motives. He had simply been required to reply to two or three plain factual questions. Not only had all the work been done by Warden but all the strain had been carried by him too. In fact, in spite of the awe-inspiring position he had been placed in, high and lifted up in lonely eminence before the judge, Bernard could not feel that he'd been through a strenuous or exacting test. He'd been apprehensive rather than fearful or tense. He wouldn't wish to enter that box very often; he left it with a feeling of relief.

Back in his pew, he leaned over to Warden. "Thank you. I'm terribly grateful. I should have been hopeless on my own."

"No one is ever up there on his own."

"You did all the work for me."

"That's what I'm employed to do."

"I suppose I owe thanks to Godfreys'."

"You do."

"Quiet!" rapped the clerk, stilling the general hum that had arisen. "Any more objections?"

Silence prevailed. The judge put on some spectacles and peered around the court. Still there was silence. Was it that no one else had come with a mind to object? Or was it that Warden's display of forensic skill had left others unwilling to challenge it? Whatever, the silence continued. The judge motioned to the clerk below, who handed up a funny-shaped hat that looked like a cross between a tea cozy and a miniature Noah's ark. The judge put it on his head.

"In that case," he declaimed, "I formally confirm the claimant,

Bernard Dayman, as an accredited applicant for a house in the New Town, with a right to immediate enrollment on the Waiting List. The court is adjourned."

The judge rose and left while all stood quiet. Then there was an outbreak of chatter and movement. In the midst of it, the clerk of the court, with great agility, vaulted rapidly over all the benches and partitions between his seat and the door.

"A remarkable man," Warden said. "He never deviates. Straight as a die. You cannot deflect him from his course."

He put a friendly arm on Bernard's shoulder as they left the courtroom. Bernard tried to find some words of gratitude.

"You were wonderful. Terribly skillful."

"They almost found a chink in your armor, Bernard. Almost. It was a near thing. Let me advise you to get hold of some New Town literature as soon as possible."

How Bernard and Marie attended a meeting of the Society of Waiters, and how they participated in the rites and ceremonies

Two days after Bernard's hearing, he and Marie received identical communications through the post. They learned that, by being enrolled on the Waiting List, they were automatically elected members of the Society of Waiters. This association had been founded "to foster the virtue of patience and the spirit of fellowship among those looking forward to residence in the New Town and to encourage those still not nominated to the List to persist in their efforts to get themselves formally accepted."

The work of encouraging outsiders was a matter of approaching them with "help, sympathy, fellowship, and information about the New Town and its inhabitants."

There was much more in the same vein on the list of aims printed in minute type on the back of the little blue membership card. In view of what had been said at his hearing, Bernard noted with some interest that the society ran a publishing business that specialized in "literature about the New Town, its inception, its history, its personalities, and its present social and cultural life."

Of more immediate appeal was an accompanying notice of the next meeting of the local chapter of the Society of Waiters, to be held in the Hertham waiting room on the very next evening at 7:30. "Refreshments, business, discussion. All local Waiters welcome."

"Where is this waiting room?" Bernard asked.

"It's the double-fronted Gothic-style building in Market Street, just opposite Godfreys'," Marie said.

"Surely that's far too grand a building to be a waiting room."

"Not if you take the words in the right sense. The members of the Society are people who regard having their names on the Waiting List as the most important thing about their current position in Hertham. When you consider how unsatisfying life is in the Old Town, you can see their point. They pride themselves on being Waiters and naturally regard their meeting place as dedicated to waiting."

"I see. Are you going to the meeting?"

"Of course. So are you."

"I shall be the most untutored Waiter present."

"I'm sure they allow for that. I'm told that new members have to keep quiet at first till they learn what is the right thing to say in the society's little formal ceremonies. To begin with you're what's called a 'dumb Waiter.' But that doesn't last for long."

At the meeting Bernard only gradually began to understand the Society's ways. He and Marie were welcomed at the door by a dark-suited, cherubic-looking young man with bright eyes and a confident manner.

"I'm John," he said, "and I'm happy to be looking after you on your first evening. Enjoy!"

Looking around, Bernard took stock of their surroundings. The hall would have held two hundred people comfortably on the chairs arranged along the walls. Down the middle of the room ran a long line of tables covered with white cloths and laden with sandwiches, cakes, plates, cups, glasses, and drinks. People stood around chatting in groups until, at 7:30 promptly, someone rang a little bell. At once the entire gathering formed up in single file. The leader stood at the top end of the tables, and the line behind him stretched round the edges of the room. At a second tinkle of the bell, the entire gathering fell silent.

"Why are we waiting?" the head Waiter chanted in a kind of plainsong.

"We're waiting for homes," the rest replied as one.

After a slight pause, the head Waiter chanted again.

"Why are we waiting?"

"We are waiting for food," the members replied.

The bell tinkled again; they moved in procession around the buffet tables, and all in turn helped themselves to platefuls of food.

"Don't eat yet," John said to Bernard and Marie, clinging to them as they moved about. "Watch what we do, and do the same."

After they had all helped themselves, they withdrew from the tables a few yards and stood still. There was a tinkle from the bell, and the head Waiter chanted once more. "Why are we waiting?"

"We are waiting because we are Waiters," the rest replied in singsong tones. At once all of them offered their plates to their neighbors, as though they were indeed waiters waiting on them. And in turn they all took one delicacy from their neighbors' plates.

There was another tinkle, and at once the gathering relaxed into informality. They ate. They returned to the table to collect drinks. They chatted together in groups.

"It looks as though the formalities are over," Bernard said to Marie.

"Not yet," John said. "There's more to come."

Indeed the bell tinkled again as refreshments were over, and another formal ceremony took place. All the members present sat down on the chairs along the walls. From a side room the head Waiter came in. He had the air of a professional restaurateur. There was a white napkin over the left arm of his evening suit, and on his head he wore a chef's white hat. He was followed by a uniformed Waitress, carrying a large cardboard box on a silver tray. The two of them processed slowly right around the room, pausing before each member in turn, and the head Waiter took chocolates from the box and handed one to each with a graceful bow. Last of all, the head Waiter put the box on the table and took one himself. Again the bell tinkled. Everyone stood up, and they all popped their chocolates into their mouths with their right hands and ate them.

This was the last of the ceremonies directly connected with the buffet. As the gathering relaxed once more into informality, John turned to Bernard and Marie and gave each of them a card.

"You need to read these," he said, "or the ceremony doesn't make sense."

Bernard studied his card. It had verses under the heading "The Waiter's Song" on the back and an explanatory paragraph about chocolates on the front.

SHARING CHOCOLATES

The Society of Waiters has always celebrated the memory of the founder by recalling one of his most significant gestures, a gesture that was indicative of his immense generosity. Christopher Godfrey, of course, firmly refused to restrict his activities within the business circles to which he properly belonged.

The most impressive act of his career, perhaps, was his decision to go slumming for a period with down-and-outs, sleeping at night in a cardboard box in a shop doorway, while working by day as a waiter in the meanest of institutions, a canteen for pig minders, in which it was said that there was often little to differentiate what was fed to the animals from what was fed to their keepers. When an admirer tracked him down and presented him with a huge box of chocolates, what did he do but go around the whole of the inner city area of destitution, tramping from one shop doorway to another, offering his chocolates to the dropouts until the box was empty?

Later, when this gesture had become common knowledge, the company's board of directors established the practice of passing a box of chocolates around after every formal meeting. And when the Society of Waiters was established, the board set up an endowment to make the practice permanent. Under its terms, confectionery manufactured in the New Town Chocolate Factory shall be made freely available to all members of the Society of Waiters at all meetings held here in Old Hertham. Every member of the Society is asked to take and eat a chocolate in memory of the Society's founder and benefactor.

"Young Godfrey put everything he had into the Society," John explained. "It was a waste of resources, some people say. They make out that he almost ruined the firm by endowing the Society."

At that point a pianist struck a chord and everyone stood up. "Let us sing 'The Waiter's Song,'" the head Waiter intoned in a firm voice, at which the assembled members all rose to their feet.

> I love to be a waiter,
> To serve while others feed,
> To bring the plate and cater
> To every diner's need.
> I serve the steaming plateful
> Of steak and kidney pie,
> Happy to see the grateful
> Smile in every eye.
>
> These etiquettes are followed
> In Hertham's aging town.
> I see the liquids swallowed;
> I watch the food go down.
> Yet as I serve hot dishes
> Or ices from the fridge,
> My dearest hopes and wishes
> Take wing across the bridge.

New Hertham is the venue
For the discerning guest,
Where every day the menu
Contains the very best,
Where even as a beginner,
The chance may yet be mine
To serve Sir Alph at dinner
And fill his glass with wine.

After the singing came the "business." This was a brief interlude during which certain announcements were made, not all of which made sense to Bernard and Marie. Some, however, were clear enough. A few names were read of Waiters and Waitresses who had recently "passed on to higher service in the New Town." Members were urged not to forget them entirely but to keep in touch by occasionally sending a postcard.

"Those who are no longer with us," the head Waiter said, "may be much helped in their new life by being able to feel that they have our sympathy and support as much as ever. Besides, some of them may already have the ear of people on the Allocation Committee, and may be able to put in a useful word for us at the right moment."

An election followed, for among those recently departed to the New Town was a lady in waiting who had to be replaced. John explained that gentlemen in waiting and ladies in waiting were officers of the Society concerned with the Society's overall direction, policy, and propaganda. It was their responsibility to elect the head Waiter from among their body.

The "discussion" that followed the "business" was opened by the head Waiter.

"For my brief homily this evening, I'm taking as my text a familiar expression: 'Wait for it!' I heard it used only yesterday by a man raising his finger and bidding his friends prepare to hear an astonishing announcement.

"Waiters and Waitresses, you do not need me to tell you that the word *wait* is most often used of exercising patience and keeping calm. You have to wait for your train in the morning. You may have to wait for your supper in the evening. You wait your turn in the taxi queue. Children have to wait patiently for their birthdays, for Christmas, for their school vacations. We urge the person to wait patiently who is eagerly looking forward to some hoped-for pleasure or fretfully restless because some payment or reward has been delayed. This is an exhortation to someone to be calm and steady and to keep eagerness and anticipation in check.

"But was this what our friend was urging yesterday when he raised his finger and said, 'Wait for it!'? On the contrary, he was as good as saying, 'Prepare yourselves! Hold yourselves ready, for the exciting thing is just about to happen!' This was not an exhortation to people to restrain their hopes and expectations. It was a message stoking up their anticipation to fever pitch. Indeed 'Wait for it!' marked the end of the waiting game.

"I've used this little illustration of contrasting usages of the word *wait* because I think it provides a parable of what it means to be a Waiter. We must all wait in the sense that we must be patient and calm, that we must not be restless or fretful under the strains of delay or deferment. We must trust quietly in the promised security of eventual residence in the New Town. Yet at the same time, it is our duty to 'wait for it' in the opposite sense. We must prepare ourselves and hold ourselves in readiness; we must be poised in eager anticipation of the immense delight awaiting us at the moment when the call comes for us to move into the New Town. For it may come at any time.

"The paradox of the Waiter's calling is that he must respond to these seemingly contradictory demands at the same time. The good Waiter is, by the very nature of his situation in Hertham, a person in a state of tension, a person practicing the discipline of quiet patience, yet also a person agog with enthusiasm for that which he anticipates. And not only anticipates, for the very flavor of residence in the New Town is tasted as we study the NT books and meditate on what lies ahead of us if we are faithful. We cannot but be excited and elated when we hear that, among those who have gone before us, there are some who not only enjoy the full amenities of life in a modern town equipped with all that is best but also have the special professional privilege of waiting upon the lord mayor himself at one of his frequent official banquets, offering the hors d'oeuvre or the dessert to the great Sir Alph Godfrey in person.

"You may wonder why I've touched upon this particular theme this evening. It's because there has lately been a good deal of controversy in the press, most of it highly critical of our attitude as Waiters. They say we gather together to eat chocolates and drink coffee while floors are rotting under people's feet. It is true that we do. That's what chocolates and coffee are for. You cannot prop up floorboards with chocolate and cure dry rot by spraying joists with coffee. I may add that I have not observed

135

any notable abstinence from either chocolates or coffee among the critics of our society.

"There's more to waiting, however, than either patience or expectancy. Our ceremonies speak of a different mode of waiting. Service is a keynote of our society. We serve one another by waiting on one another whenever we meet, proffering food in humility each to each. The poet summed it up comprehensively when he wrote, 'They also wait who only stand and serve.'"

A ripple of applause ended the head Waiter's address, followed by a few moments of that embarrassed silence and stillness in which an audience waits for someone to break the ice by asking a question or making a point.

Eventually a quiet-spoken man gently raised his hand. "Sir, I should like to raise a very topical issue. I had a long argument with a neighbor of mine last week. He complained that we in the Society use a vocabulary and a set of concepts that no longer mean anything to those outside. For instance, he said, take the business of calling yourselves Waiters and dressing up as such. That might have been fine in the days when waiters were to be found all over the place in shops and cafés, but nowadays you rarely meet a waiter. Waiting of that kind has almost gone. This is the age of self-service. Wherever you go now in Hertham, shopping or eating out, indeed even filling up your car with gas, you will find self-service operating. People who criticize our society are surely right when they say that since self-service has replaced waiting, we should reexpress our Society's ethos in terms of self-service rather than of waiting. This would meet the needs of people today."

"But it would change the whole meaning of the Society," a lady objected. "Waiting and self-service are totally different things."

"That's beside the point," the male voice continued. "You cannot get in touch with people if you talk what to them is a lot of mumbo-jumbo or if you continually use images and symbols that belong to ancient history."

"I can't go all the way with this kind of talk," another man said, "but there is something in it. Perhaps we should overhaul some of our imagery and try to express our truths in contemporary terms. Last week when I talked to a dear friend of mine and referred to a lady in waiting, she thought I was referring to an expectant mother."

"That's nothing," someone interjected. "My hairdresser thinks a lady in waiting is an expensive call girl."

"Some of these mistakes are natural," the head Waiter said. "We ought to use the opportunities they offer us for pressing our message home. We can do so if we have our wits about us. After all, there is a sense in which each one of us is expectant and each one of us should be always on call. That's a fine note on which to finish tonight. We can take that thought away with us for quiet reflection. Let us end by singing the Society anthem, 'Blessed Township.'"

At that, the company arose and once more gave voice with gusto:

Blessed township, Hertha Nova,
Where the faithful find their rest,
Where enjoyment bubbles over
Because there is no second best.

Simple souls and learned sages,
The stinking rich, the humble poor,
Pensioners and single parents
There unite for evermore.

There no fungus rots the timbers,
No workings undermine the town,
Roads maintain their proper level,
Pavements never let you down.
There unknown is faulty plumbing,
Floors are firm and walls are dry.
Hail the end of worm and beetle,
Falling slates and DIY!

Air-conditioned, central heating,
Double glazing, parquet floors,
En suite bathrooms, fitted kitchens,
Loggias with sliding doors.
Oh, how glorious is the prospect
Opened up to waiting men,
To waiting women, waiting children,
Waiting cats and dogs! Amen.

The singing done, the members rose to go.

Before leaving the waiting room at the end of the proceedings, Bernard and Marie lingered at the newsstand that occupied a corner of the hall. It carried a large and varied stock of books, pamphlets, and brochures about the New Town layout, the design and equipment of houses, the special arrangements

138

for social and communal activities, and the amenities available for culture, recreation, and amusement. There were also biographical studies of New Town personalities, accounts of the growth and development of the New Town project, and many more technical books on aspects of architecture and problems of engineering. Mixed up with forbidding-looking technical titles were seemingly less demanding booklets such as *The Waiter's Progress, The Old Man and the New Town, Mere Newness, The New Mind, and Godfrey and the Chocolate Factory.*

Partly out of a sense of duty, and partly out of sheer curiosity, Bernard and Marie purchased a number of books.

"Before we get home," Marie said, "we may begin to wish we hadn't burdened ourselves with these."

She spoke more truly than she knew, for two people walking home together in the darkness, Bernard discovered, can be circumscribed in their movements when each carries an armful of books. Bernard carried his under his left arm, Marie hers in her right hand. Marie walked on Bernard's right and was able to take his right arm, as he had thrust his right hand deep into his pocket in order to counterbalance the burden on the other side.

Somehow hands and arms were as fully occupied as they could have been; impulsive, amorous improvisation seemed ruled out in advance.

Walking at Marie's side, glimpsing the clarity of her profile in the lamplight and the mystery of it in the shadows, Bernard felt strangely teased, almost tantalized. Four hands, four arms, four legs, safely involved in a pattern of action that it would be awkward and clumsy to break. Of course, it was a delight to be taken into the rhythm of their joint progress. Yet something dragged at Bernard to break out of it—something that Marie's face, at one moment in the blackness, at the next in brightness, achingly abetted.

It was a beautiful, still autumn night. Way up the hill ahead of them there was a richness of tone in the sky that gave a peculiar clarity to the gap between the first skyline and the second skyline, between suburban chimney pot and remote hilltop.

"It's as though a bit of sunset has been left behind," Bernard said. "The sky there seems to speak of something that has gone."

"Or of something to come," Marie mused.

They moved through many slight fluctuations of mood, through many gradations of apprehension, mystification, conjecture, fear, and uncertainty between that first moment of strange pleasure at a glow in the sky and the moment when they stood, still and speechless, staring at Netherhome Lodge wrapped in flames.

How Bernard and Marie weathered ordeal by fire, and
how a dream chastened Eve

Bad as it was, it might have been a lot worse. It was the single-story section of the cottage that burned fiercely, and the firemen were plainly trying to contain the blaze in that section.

Bernard tried to sound appreciative of their efforts as he approached one of the firemen. "There seems to be a good chance that you will save the other half of the building."

"It's what we're trying to do. And we may well manage it. That's a solid stone wall up the middle, you know. It must have been an outside wall once. I reckon this part that's burning was built later than the rest."

Eve leaned against the roadside wall opposite the cottage with her thick coat wrapped around her. "I can't think how it happened. I've always been so careful. I was sitting still, reading the paper, when suddenly I smelled burning. Then there was a crackling noise above me. None of us smokes. There hasn't been a match struck in there all day."

The fireman shook his head knowingly. "I can tell you how it started. One look was enough for me. You've got a rotten roof, haven't you?"

"She had yesterday," Marie said.

"Well, she had then. And I'll tell you something else she had. She had rotten wiring up there. Isn't that right?"

Bernard nodded.

"That's the nicest little combination you can have. Rotten wood and rotten wiring in a nice cozy little roof where no one can see what's happening." The fireman seemed to take pleasure in the happy coincidence. "Woof! Up she goes. It happens somewhere every day."

"But it was so quick," Eve said. "One moment a bit of a smell, and then next moment it was like this. As soon as I got out of there, the whole roof was in flames."

"As quick as that, was it? Shall I tell you why?"

They waited for him to do so.

"You see that break in the roof near the junction? Several slates were missing there."

Bernard knew only too well. Those were the slates he had brought down in his clumsy attempt to patch the roof.

"That hole did it."

"What do you mean?" Bernard felt that he was being made responsible.

"Draft. That's what I mean. Draft. There was just enough of it. Not too much and not too little." The fireman grinned, seemingly happy at having another fruitful coincidence to relish. "The wiring burned through, and the wood caught. It might have smoldered and gone out. It might have smoked until the lady here noticed it and called us up on the phone. We could have put it right soon enough at that stage. But it didn't just smolder, and it didn't just smoke, because there was that convenient hole, just the right size and in just the right place. The draft was ready-made. So the thing flamed." The fireman turned to Eve. "Whoever left you with that hole left you with a load of trouble."

"It was patched," Marie said, coming to Bernard's aid.

"With what?"

"Roofing felt," Bernard said faintly.

"Roofing felt, was it?" The fireman laughed. "I thought you were going to say newspaper."

Bernard's heart sank, but the fireman plowed on, plainly enjoying himself.

"That hole was a built-in fireplace. And that roofing felt, when it curled up in the heat, made a nice little draft screen. It channeled the air flow from underneath till the fire really got going. My grandmother used to hold a sheet of newspaper over the fireplace till the kindling wood blazed. Then, when the fire was really going, she whipped the paper away. And when this fire was really going, the roofing felt melted and curled, and the full draft was let in. It might have been all specially designed. Built-in fireplace," he went on, obviously relishing his own cleverness. "Built-in fireplace, and built-in draft screen as an optional extra."

Within two hours of Bernard's and Marie's arrival on the scene, the fire was out, the brigade gone, the road cleared, and the damage inspected. All this was astonishing to Bernard. The layman, seeing the blaze of an hour or two ago, would have assumed that the fire would take a lot of handling and that the whole cottage might quickly be gutted. In fact, however, the two-story section of the building remained intact. This meant that their dining room, kitchen, and bedrooms were all usable, all protected by the solid wall and the firemen's skill. The damage was confined to the single-story section. What hurt most was that they had lost their lovely sitting room.

Eve, who at first bore the evening's shock with surprising calm, showed signs of faintness when they were able to return inside. Bernard and Marie had to help her up to her bedroom and lay her to rest on her bed, where she soon fell asleep. It was then that Bernard and Marie, moving about the comparatively undamaged portion of the house in an atmosphere of incongruous normality, were able to take stock of the situation.

Even in the single-story section of the building, the scene wasn't as desolate as they had expected. The insecurity of the slates on their worn-out nails, such a nuisance in the past, had proved an advantage now. The slates had slid down as the fire took hold, shuddering off the roof into the garden. They had not, for the most part, fallen into the house. Their weight being removed, the roof beams had not crashed heavily down into the house either. Though charred and damp, some of them were still in place.

Bernard and Marie stood there and stared up at the few re-maining wooden beams, gaunt and jagged against the night sky. Bernard pointed upward.

"Look at those two beams sticking up like a memorial cross!"

"Yes," Marie said. "It was nail weariness that saved us from an even more disastrous fall."

As she and Bernard stood there on the squelchy carpet, with bits of charred wood scattered around damp but undamaged table legs, and with a layer of sodden ash under their feet, they realized that a rescue operation on one or two nice pieces of furniture was perfectly possible, and it was some time later, after a hard bout of cleaning and drying, that they returned to the dining room.

Here they were pleasantly surprised to find that Eve had come downstairs, made a pot of tea and some sandwiches, and lit candles and a fire.

"Electricity is out for the present," she said. "It seems odd to be comforting oneself by staring at flames. Anyway, sit down and have something to eat. I'm not sure whether it's a late nightcap or an early breakfast."

"I'll just wash my hands first," Bernard said, following Marie into the kitchen.

Returning some moments later, he found Eve gazing placidly at the fire. He laid his soaking shoes on the hearth. As he sat at the table, Marie returned.

"I've something to tell you," Eve said suddenly. "I've changed my mind. I've decided that you're right."

Bernard and Marie looked at her in some surprise, waiting for more.

"I was wrong. You can't make a permanent home in Hertham. You're up against too much."

This news was received in silence. Eve's words represented a complete U-turn. And yet, to Bernard, the most astonishing thing about them was that they did not really astonish him. Rather, they seemed natural, unforced. It was as though the present situation cried out for this kind of utterance, and Eve supplied it.

"It all started yesterday," Eve said. "They brought poor Professor Simpkins into the hospital in a terrible state. I had to be

145

there as usual to record the reception details. He's had a complete breakdown, and he won't have anything to do with any of the doctors who want to help him. He calls the psychiatrists 'sky pietists,' and he seems to think he's on the stage. He lies on his back declaiming speeches and singing something about 'doing it my way.' The sight of it shook me a bit and prepared the ground, I suppose. Tonight has really taught me a lesson. I've been lying in bed thinking. You can't go on pretending a place is just the same when it changes as this cottage has changed. That's what's wrong with the Preservation Trust. The Hertham it tries to save isn't there anymore. It's in your mind, but it doesn't exist outside. The Hertham that does exist is terribly insecure. I find it hard to explain. The thing is personal, really. You've made a great change for me, Bernard. It's partly your coming that has done it."

"How have I changed things? You mean that I bungled it when I tried to mend the roof and made sure that a fire would spread quickly once it took hold? I'm sorry about that, of course."

"No, no. You mustn't think I'm saying that. Anyway, I'm grateful for the fire now. You see, when you came I thought perhaps I could still be the girl you fell in love with. Of course, I couldn't. I'd changed too much. I pictured myself as a certain person, when in fact that person ceased to exist a long time ago. By what you said and did, I think you tried to make me see myself. But I didn't fully see myself. Not until tonight. I can see myself now. I'm the human counterpart of Old Hertham. I'm Netherhome Lodge in the flesh."

"You're not," Bernard protested. "Not burnt out. Not even half burnt out. Certainly not decaying. I can't allow that."

146

"Let me put it like this, Bernard. I got really keen on the Preservation Trust. But now I think it was all because of the gap between my picture of this cottage and what it had actually become. The roof rotted and the floor rotted, and they had to prop up the walls and bridge a hole in the garden, but nevertheless, my picture of the place didn't really change. Tonight half the building was destroyed by fire, but when I first came in and saw that this part was more or less untouched, I found myself saying, 'Good. It's still my beloved home.' Then later, as I lay on the bed, I began to ask myself, 'Suppose the place is struck by another act of God, or whatever they call it; what then?'

"Well, I dropped off to sleep, and I had a most vivid dream. I still lay where I was, but the rooms around me were peeled off one by one. I could see it happening, even though I was in the middle of it. I was inside myself and outside myself at the same time. The other rooms were peeled off till there was only my bedroom left, floating in midair with me lying on the bed in the middle of it. Outside there was nothing but a post standing in a bare field, with the sign 'Netherhome Lodge' hanging on it. That wasn't the end either. The walls of my bedroom were peeled away next, then the floor, the ceiling, the bed, the bedclothes, and finally my own clothes. All that was left was me, naked, floating in the air, and a notice 'Netherhome Lodge' floating there too. It doesn't tax the brain much to make sense of a dream like that. I shall have to get on that Waiting List."

Later Marie went to bed, and Bernard was able to talk to Eve alone. He was glad of the opportunity—glad of it for the first time since he had met Marie. Why did he now want an intimacy that he had lately been at pains to avoid? Was it that Eve had now, after her recantation, become the Eve of his boyhood again?

Looking at her face now, caught midway between the flickering light from the fire and the steady glow from the candle on the table, Bernard saw again, in the still outline of her profile and in the unsteady, darting of light and blackness across her features, that blend of clarity and mystery that had lured and teased him long ago. Momentarily she was once more the Eve who had sat beside him in the cinema as a girl of sixteen.

"Well?"

When she turned toward him and spoke, the image was broken. There was too much in the history of those eyes and that voice in which he had no part. Neither Marie's face nor Marie's expression ever gave him that sense of a weight of act and fact that belonged to someone else. Yet he was not now alienated by the recognition. Rather, he was touched as one is sometimes touched by the hint of suffering in some totally unknown face. He came and sat on the edge of the table behind her and put his arm on her shoulder.

"Eve, I'm sorry I've been so thoughtless."

"Thoughtless? When?"

"When you tried to bring back the past."

Eve shook her head. "I was the thoughtless one then."

"I was unkind."

"No."

Bernard felt that he was failing in some primary duty. Her monosyllable response sounded empty. He had brought her no comfort. How could he make amends? He leaned forward and kissed her on the cheek.

"That's kind," she said, "but I think you ought to reserve your kisses for Marie." After a moment's silence, she added, "Bernard, I did love Roger. He's Marie's father. Besides, I can be sure of one thing: if he goes on driving, it won't be long before he's up here."

The joy that Bernard had of Marie, and the grievous blow that followed

After the hearing, after the Waiters' chapter meeting, after the fire at Netherhome Lodge, and after Eve's recantation, Bernard was seized by impatience. So much seemed to have happened, yet his basic situation hadn't changed. There they were, Eve and Marie and himself, still at Netherhome Lodge, whose very fabric was disintegrating day by day.

Bernard decided to take an afternoon walk in the hills to see if the fresh air would clear his mind and stimulate him to plan the next move. He strode along the path behind the cottage. It led up the lower slopes of David's Pike, a hill that seemed to have derived its name from the fact that its top was shaped like a harp. He and Marie had walked some way up the path on the day when the dry stone wall collapsed under the pressure of their embrace. Somehow that accident epitomized his frustrations.

The positive thing was that he and Marie were now both on the Waiting List. But what did that mean? How many hundreds, thousands, of people had their names on that list and were still stuck in Old Hertham with floors collapsing beneath them and roofs showering them with rain? What were his chances, what were Marie's chances, of being able to move up to a favorable position on the List? Was it really a question of moving up? On what basis were houses in the New Town allocated?

The weather seemed to share his unsettled mood. Although he had set off in sunshine, the sky darkened as he walked, and clouds lowered over the hill he had meant to climb. He decided to go down into the town rather than risk being caught in a storm on the heights.

It was a good thing. He'd just reached the middle of the town when a sudden heavy burst of rain drove him into a shop doorway. The darkness deepened ominously. The rain fell faster and heavier till people were talking of a cloudburst. Water swirled over the sidewalks and down the road. Fellow refugees from the downpour muttered gravely that the river wouldn't be able to take it, that the Market Street cellars would soon be deep in water.

Bernard soon decided that waiting for the rain to stop was as frustrating as waiting for a house in the New Town. He decided to make the best of it. He trudged back to Netherhome Lodge over roads turned into temporary rivers. He was thoroughly drenched to the skin well before he finally reached home.

When he actually got there, he felt that Netherhome Lodge, damaged as it was, had never seemed more delightful. The rain still danced on the ground all around it, but inside all was warmth and comfort. Marie sat toasting crumpets by the fireside. Supper was ready on the table. The coke-fired boiler had gotten the bathwater roaring hot, Marie said. Bernard got out of his soaked clothes, had a quick bath, and came down to a room glowing with such important delights—fire, silver teapot, knives and forks, and china—and smelling so delectably of burning wood, toasted crumpets, and Marie's perfume that the problems that had driven him on his restless, lonely walk suddenly seemed remote and intangible. He put his hands on Marie's shoulders from behind.

"Your mother has given me permission to kiss you."

"How thoughtful of her."

"In fact, she virtually ordered me to kiss you."

"I'm overwhelmed."

"You'll be an obedient daughter, I hope."

"Yes." Without turning, she raised her hands to his on her shoulders. "Later on."

"Be serious for a minute, Marie. Your mother did speak as I said. And you know, it was her way of declaring me redundant to her needs. She's given me the golden handshake."

Marie remained silent. Bernard could not see her face. He bent over and lightly kissed her head. How could he find the right tone, the right idiom, for what he was trying to tell her?

"What I'm trying to say, Marie, is that, for my part, there never was any feeling to justify what happened. I mean the seeming wish for a ménage à trois."

Marie replied without turning her head. "I know, Bernard. Had I not known, we should not have been the friends we are."

She rose, went over to the table, and sat down presidentially at the tea-dispensing end.

Eve herself joined them a few moments later. She was relaxed and cheerful. Bernard thought relations between the three of them had never been so easy and so delightful. Eve said she had already been thinking hard about her future.

"To what effect, Mother?"

"Well, all the housing problems look different to me now."

"That doesn't tell us much."

"What matters is that I've found my way of dealing with all the frustrations." Eve spoke brightly and gave an indulgent little smile, implying that she was keeping some of her thoughts to herself.

"Since we're all so agreeably not laying our cards on the table," Bernard said, "let me say that I've been thinking things over too."

"With what result?" Marie asked.

"No change at all."

"We're blinded with enlightenment," Marie said.

"What does it matter, anyway?" Bernard lifted his hands in a gesture of sheer pleasure. He wanted to say, but felt that it would be treachery to say, that the New Town itself scarcely seemed desirable, let alone necessary, when Old Hertham could still provide even its restless residents with evenings of delight such as this one.

If he felt so during the meal, how much more did he feel so later in the evening, when supper things had been cleared away, when Eve had gone up to her room, and when Marie had sat down on the rug before the fire. For once, she took up neither a book nor her knitting but made it felt that she was ready to chat and reflect as Bernard might wish.

The inner coziness and stillness were intensified by the sound of rising wind and heavy rain outside. The windowpanes rattled; the rain beat against them incessantly. In addition to the usual storm noises of wind in the trees and in the chimneys, there were some new sound effects that Bernard mentally located in the ruined shell of the burnt-out sitting room, to which they were attached here in their comparatively solid little fortress. A strange whine, mechanical rather than bestial, he put down to the wind rushing through the gaps of the shell where the roof, the door, and the windows had been. An occasional thud he interpreted as the falling of wood or masonry from the damaged walls. He did not go out to investigate these noises. Though he regarded the ruin as safe in normal weather conditions, he knew that a wind such as tonight's might dislodge substantial pieces of the shattered fabric. He did not fancy having a hundredweight of stone dropped on his head.

Meanwhile, inside all was warmth, physical and emotional. Marie was happy to be kissed. She accepted that he loved her, agreed that she loved him, and at one point even ran her fingers through his hair, standing behind him, and said a lot by saying nothing at all as she did so. Not long before bedtime, she held his cheeks between her hands for a few moments and quietly whispered, "We shall get there, Bernard, in our due time."

Bernard wanted to reply, "Never mind getting there, and never mind the New Town. This is good enough for me!" But he was afraid of mocking or hurting Marie, so he kept quiet.

Before they went upstairs, they looked out the kitchen window at the back. Water was pouring down the lane from the hillside, running past the cottage in a stream inches deep. Stones and pebbles were carried down in it, and they knocked against the wall of the cottage, making a noise rather like that of the sea beating against cliffs.

"It's easy to imagine what damage heavy flooding can do in a

155

mountainous district," Bernard said. "I'm glad there isn't a dam up there on David's Pike."

"As a matter of fact, there is a dam," Marie said, "a small one. But it has stood up to plenty of bad nights in its time."

Bernard took her hands just before they went up to bed. "I don't think either of us will sleep much tonight, Marie." He looked in her eyes and raised his eyebrows as if he were asking a question.

"Probably not," she said brusquely, disengaging herself and making for the staircase.

Actually, Bernard had a disturbed rather than a restless night. From time to time he was awakened. Each time, he thought perhaps he had heard a thud. He listened for some moments to the water still running past the house and the pebbles still washing against the walls. But he soon fell asleep again.

The last time he awakened it was to hear a great crash that shook the house. He jumped out of bed, threw on his bathrobe, and made for the window. Dawn was breaking now, and as he opened the curtains, he expected to see evidence of new subsi-dence. Indeed the shaking of the house had been so frightening that he would not have been surprised to see that another massive chasm had opened up in the earth outside. In fact, there was at first nothing to see except the water still pouring past the house, though it now flowed much more swiftly and heavily. It looked feet deep. Then suddenly, just below the house, he noticed an enormous boulder jammed against the wall in a gateway to a field. The rock was about six feet high and as near spherical as a natural rock was likely to be. Plainly, it had been carried down the hill by the water, and seemingly, it had crashed against the wall of Netherhome Lodge before bouncing off and coming to rest on the opposite side of the lane. The curve in the lane and the steepness of the gradient had turned the wall of Netherhome Lodge into a breakwater. The rock must have crashed against it with terrific force. Small wonder that the house had been shaken. Bernard only hoped that no further serious damage had been done to the fabric.

As he turned from the window, the door opened and Marie came in looking white and frightened. Evidently, she had jumped out of bed shocked and but half aware. She was wearing only her nightgown.

"What is it, Bernard?"

"It's all right. It's all right."

"But it sounded terrible." Marie shivered and shuddered.

"No, no." Bernard took her in his arms, and she clung to him.

"I was dreaming, I think. I must have been. I thought it was the end of everything."

Still she trembled. Bernard held her tightly.

"You've had a shock, Marie, but it's all right. The water is pouring down the lane, and a great boulder has just come down with it. Netherhome Lodge was in the way and got a good bash. That's all."

"The dam!"

"I suppose so. But you said it was a small one."

"Yes." She breathed deeply. He put his hand to her head comfortingly. "I'm sorry," she added, then smiled, reassured.

"For what? Don't be sorry, Marie. I like you when you cling to me."

She looked up into his eyes. It seemed to be the moment Bernard had waited for for so long. She was at last fully held in his arms, responsive and uninhibited. Together they entered on a long, long kiss.

"Entered on" only. There was a sudden tearing, crumbling noise, and they found themselves no longer enclosed in a cozy, private bedroom, but uncovered to the sharp morning air. The side wall of the bedroom had been whipped away as though it were the curtain of a proscenium stage. The guilty actors, embracing between the scenes, were exposed to the auditorium. Fortunately, the auditorium was empty. But the awareness of a sudden uncovering was like a slap in the face to both of them. Marie buried her face in her hands in shame. Bernard saw his own overindulgent protectiveness revealed for the self-conscious drama it was and was no less ashamed. To shame was added a sense of the farcical, which was bitter at first.

"Will the house hold?" Marie asked.

"I don't care if it doesn't."

"You do, Bernard."

"All right, I do. But I'm sick of the bloody place."

"The wall must have been damaged."

"Damaged! I should say so." Bernard looked out through the gap it had left. "A large chunk of it seems to have gone down into the lane."

"Just when we needed it most."

"Just when we needed it most," Bernard agreed.

He took a blanket from the bed and threw it over Marie's shoulders. She pulled it around herself, holding it like a shawl. Bernard looked her in the eyes with a wry smile, sharing with her a common recognition of the irony of their position. From being deliciously accessible, she had suddenly become teasingly remote. He turned to look through the six-foot-wide hole in the wall at the lane and the fields and the gable end of the cottage next to theirs.

"Our relationship has become very public, Marie."

"Yes. We're on show, you might say."

"I prefer privacy."

"Don't we all?"

"Not solitary privacy, of course."

"Sometimes it's nice. There are occasions when I like to keep myself to myself."

"I'm not with you there, Marie. I like to keep yourself to myself."

He ventured a step forward, nearer the gaping hole.

"By the way, I wonder what's holding the floor up?"

"The inside walls, I suppose."

"It's funny to discover that an outside wall is not so indispensable after all."

"It made quite a difference to us, Bernard. I must go and get dressed."

"When you've done so, I'll come and get dressed too. I don't fancy dressing in public here. Oh, this place! It's always letting us down."

"The odd thing is," Marie said, looking at the floor, "that we haven't actually been let down this time."

"You win." Bernard laughed.

"No." Marie cast her eyes at the hole as she went out. "We've been exposed."

When Bernard went outside to inspect the damage, he found that he had guessed correctly what had happened. The boulder had hit the wall of the kitchen underneath his bedroom. The main force of the impact had been upon a point about three feet above road level. Cracks in the wall, opening out downward from that point, were plainly visible. But the wall below the impact point had held and saved them from flooding. If the stones had given way over that area, the water now pouring past the house would have been pouring straight into the kitchen.

Above the point of the main impact, however, cracks opening outward and upward in the shape of the letter V had so weakened the wall that a triangular section had fallen outward. Thus there was an upwardly increasing hole toward the top of the kitchen wall and a similar but correspondingly wider one on the wall of his (strictly Marie's) bedroom above. The inside walls had held firm.

Bernard surveyed the damage with mixed feelings. It was fortunate that the outer wall had reacted to the impact with the tendency to fall outward, not inward. That the lower section of cracked and loosened wall, the section below the point of impact, had not fallen out was perhaps partly due to the pressure of the running water flooding against it. In short, the flood had at least saved them from flooding.

Eve took the new disaster with remarkable cheerfulness. She rang up the police, who took note of her call and told her to ring up the Council Engineer's Department. Eve thanked the people who took her calls so profusely that the conversations, at least as overheard by Bernard, sounded like an effusive exchange of courtesies.

"They were very nice about it," Eve said, having put down the receiver. "After all, they must be very busy this morning with emergency calls. When I said we had lost a piece of wall, the man said, 'So have other people, you know.' But he said it so good-humoredly that one couldn't take offense."

How Bernard and Marie earnestly sought Dr. Fisher to aid their quest

Bernard and Marie went to see Dr. Fisher together. He fetched an extra chair for the customer's side of the counter.

"Generally speaking, I prefer to interview my clients one at a time. Three-cornered conversations can be very confusing in business negotiations, but in the present circumstances, perhaps your interests as individuals coincide fairly closely."

"I'm sure they do," Bernard said.

"You are sure." Dr. Fisher nodded happily. "And I am always open to conviction. Good." He settled down on his stool, benign and tranquil. "What can I do for you?"

"We're not impatient," Bernard began, "but we really would like to know—"

"One moment, please!" Dr. Fisher interrupted him and turned questioningly to Marie. "I think already there may be some divergence of view between the two of you."

Marie understood the objection immediately. "All right. We are impatient," she said.

"An impasse," Dr. Fisher said. "Right at the start. A head-on collision." His voice was firm, though there was humor in his eyes.

"No," Bernard said. "I agree absolutely with Marie. We are impatient. I expressed myself badly."

"You did indeed," Dr. Fisher said, "if by 'not impatient' you really meant 'impatient.' I'm not a stickler for precise terminology as such. I hope I'm not a verbal pedant. One can't always find the mot juste, but where the choice is between opposites, it's as well to opt for the correct one."

Bernard saw that the more he beat about the bush, the more Dr. Fisher would play with him dialectically in this jocular cat-and-mouse fashion. He would have to come clean.

"How long shall we have to wait for a house in the New Town?" he asked.

"What is the next step we must take?" Marie added.

"How long is the Waiting List?"

"Who selects the new residents?"

"Have you anything to offer us?"

"Or any advice to give us?"

Dr. Fisher's eyes moved from one to the other with clockwork regularity as their questions assailed him.

"Such an outburst of frankness! I like it. In fairness I must reciprocate. Our system, after all, is a just one. There is no reason to be secretive about it. New houses are being completed every week in the New Town. As the vacancies occur, we compile short lists of candidates from the Waiting List. Short-listed candidates appear before the Allocation Committee of the Housing Department. The Committee studies every case carefully, sparing no pains over matters of detail that to the layman might at first sight seem petty or trivial. They take the maximum precautions to ensure that justice is done. All of us who have seen the committee at work agree that for painstaking attention to minutiae, for scrupulous analysis of evidence and intensive scrutiny of alleged qualifications, it is an unbeatable body, quite unbeatable. There is not the slightest possibility that anyone whose case contains the faintest trace of pretense or charlatanry will ever get it past the Allocation Committee. No, I think I can remove any possible uncertainties on that score. You need not doubt for a moment that justice is done, and every case treated on its merits by what is virtually an infallible system. Does that content you?"

"No," said Bernard, who had now learned to be frank.

"Why not?"

"It answers a question we were not asking."

"Indeed!"

"It allays doubts we never entertained," Marie added. "We've never distrusted the selection machinery. We're not asking to have its credentials guaranteed. We only want to know how it works."

"Of course." Dr. Fisher nodded his head apologetically. "And you allowed me to diverge from explanation into justification."

"On what basis is a short list compiled?" Bernard asked.

"Dear me, you have become clearheaded, Bernard. I must congratulate you and do my best to keep up with you. Short lists are compiled on the basis of an elaborate points system. The system is designed to do full justice to all relevant features of each candidate's case. That is to say, for instance, it takes into account characteristics that fall under the heading 'Assess the candidate's personal fitness for residence in the New Town, bearing in mind the high standard of its social life, the outstanding qualities of its public amenities, and the delicate adjustments of relationship necessitated by entry upon a communal venture shared by people of vastly different backgrounds and outlooks.' That is always a difficult section for agents to complete and keep up-to-date. Aided though we are by the most highly organized information service, we find the work put into the records on this particular side endlessly exacting. But I think I can assure you that justice is done."

"So we are each given points for personal fitness?" Marie asked.

"That's right. They are put down on your individual record cards. We cannot, of course, divulge the contents of the cards to anyone except the selecting authorities. Naturally, they contain much that is confidential. But there need be no secrecy about the system itself."

"What else do we get points for?" Bernard asked.

"Oh, there are innumerable sections on the record cards, for no stone is left unturned to ensure that a full picture is obtained in every case. Performance-related criteria are, of course, central to the assessment system: personal adaptability, special aptitudes, individual skills, notable limitations. We must have a balanced community, you see, and these are some of the headings that help us to build up a full and fair picture on the personal side. But of course, there are also ratings based on measurements of a more impersonal nature. Environment-related criteria have to be brought to bear. Present housing conditions, for instance, are naturally taken into account."

"Then we benefit from having lost a wing of the cottage by fire?" Marie asked.

"Twenty points."

"And from having subsidence in the garden?"

"Five points."

"And from dry rot in the floors?"

"Ten points."

"And the propped-up front wall?"

"Fifteen points."

"We have lost a sizeable portion of the end wall by flood too," Bernard said.

"Another fifteen points."

"Well, well!" Marie sighed. "There's something to be said for these disasters after all."

Bernard leaned forward. "Dr. Fisher, do you mean that we can compensate by present housing troubles for failure to accumulate points on the performance-related scale?"

"No." Dr. Fisher's tone was sharp and firm. "The aggregate of points is not of itself the decisive factor. Ratings must reach a certain minimum in all sections before a case comes up for consideration."

Bernard began to wonder where the nerve center of this machinery of assessment could possibly be. He felt now that he and Marie were trapped in a network Byzantine in its ramifications and Kafkaesque in its final inscrutability. He didn't risk his question. He just said quietly, "There seems to be an awful lot of data to be correlated."

"True," Dr. Fisher agreed. "But justice is done. Fairness in correlating candidates' ratings in the various categories is the special responsibility of our Overseer for Sifting Town Entry Details—OFSTED, as we call him."

"And when, after all this, a case does actually come up before the Allocation Committee, what are the candidate's chances of getting a home?"

"About fifty-fifty, roughly speaking. I told you that the committee does its work of sifting and examining with the utmost thoroughness."

"So for every short-listed candidate who gets a house, there is one who doesn't."

"That's about it."

"And what happens to those who don't?"

"They remain on the Waiting List, of course. Their cases may come up for reconsideration at any time. I have known cases reconsidered and rejected as many as five times. Every encouragement is given to people to persevere in their efforts. Before you go I'll give you a copy of the updated Waiter's Charter."

Bernard leaned tensely forward again, and spoke gently, very gently. "Dr. Fisher, how long is a short list?"

"About twelve names usually. The Allocation Committee meets three or four times a week. The contractors are now handing over completed houses at the rate of over a hundred a month. We hope to step up this figure before long."

"Twenty or so lucky people a week?" Marie whispered.

"That's a fairly rough figure," Dr. Fisher agreed.

"And how many names are there on the Waiting List?" Bernard asked, dragging out the words with some effort.

"You have seen the volumes," Dr. Fisher said. "I would not wish to depress you. In any case, business is so brisk with us that we have little time for what might be called 'stocktaking.' From time to time the authorities take a census, and a complete picture is obtained, though I must confess that taking a census is such a tediously protracted business that by the time its results are published, they are already out-of-date. No, I should prefer not to be pressed on that point. You can take it from me that the Waiting List is substantially overloaded, and so it should be. As agents, we naturally prefer to operate in a healthy market, but our business is to commend the New Town to all, and it would be poor salesmanship to discourage clients by stressing how long the Waiting List is and how short the short lists are. Besides, clients would draw false deductions from such comparisons. Arithmetic is a poor guide in matters of this kind. Let me assure you that there is no cause for depression."

Bernard looked at Marie.

Marie looked at Bernard.

In silence they seemed to agree that there was no cause for elation either.

It was Bernard who broke the silence, nodding his head reflectively. "You people here—you really do believe in keeping people waiting, don't you?"

Dr. Fisher nodded slowly in response. "We do indeed, Bernard. The poet put it neatly: 'If you can wait and not get tired of waiting, you'll catch the bus, my son!'"

"So those people who manage the Society of Waiters, with all their playacting, have really got a point."

"They understand what's what."

"And you approve of all that kind of thing?"

"Like all agents, I am an ex officio vice president of the Society."

"And you like the way they embellish waiting with graceful ceremonies, though waiting is wearisomely negative."

"Negative? I can't allow that. Human beings don't just wait without objective. You wait for something, or you wait upon someone. It's what you're waiting for and whom you're waiting upon that matters. We're not in the business here of just waiting vacantly or without objective. As for 'wearisome,' well, one of our ancient sages has said the last word on that: 'They that wait upon Sir Alph shall renew their strength; they shall mount up with wings as eagles, they shall run and not be weary, they shall walk and not faint.'"

These words, intoned gravely and slowly by Dr. Fisher, who held his hands formally apart, were clearly intended to make a distinct, even solemn impression. In the brief moment of silence that followed this utterance, Bernard almost felt that perhaps someone ought to say, "Amen." But the thought was brushed away by a sudden transformation in Dr. Fisher's bearing. He shifted immediately in both voice and gesture to a totally different mood and manner. "By the way," he said casually, as though adding a conversational afterthought, "I have some news for you." He dived under the counter and produced a rolled-up bunch of documents.

"These are the title deeds of Netherhome Lodge. Mrs. Knight wants me to hand them over to you."

"To me?" Marie gasped.

"To both of you jointly. She has been in to see me this morning to finalize the transaction on the legal side."

"But why is she doing this?" Bernard asked.

"She said she was feeling 'de trop.' I don't want to be personal, but I can quite understand that such might be a possible reaction by a third party in the circumstances."

"Oh no!" Marie said. "We wouldn't want her to feel that."

"I assured her that you wouldn't," Dr. Fisher said, "though, strictly speaking, it was none of my business. Yet, knowing you both as I do, I thought I could take the liberty."

"You were quite right, Dr. Fisher," Bernard said.

"And your mother did assure me in turn that in fact there was no question of her being pushed out or encouraged to make this decision by any attitude of yours. She said she wanted to leave the cottage to you, that it was her own wish and feelings that determined this decision."

"But where will she go?"

"She said she would find somewhere. She'd be better on her own for a time, she told me."

"We can't allow it," Bernard said.

"I'm afraid you can't stop it. Netherhome Lodge is Mrs. Knight's house, and she has the right to dispose of it as she wishes."

"I can't possibly think what put such an idea into her head," Marie said.

"As to that," Dr. Fisher said gravely, "she was kind enough to confide in me. Seeking advice, she had called the Christopher Godfrey Helpline. When she spoke of her situation, they told her to press number nine for the recorded message of the day, and it said, 'Christopher gave all his chocolates away.'"

"But it looks so awful," Marie said, "as though we've made her feel uncomfortable."

"It may look so," Dr. Fisher said, "but in fact it isn't so. Throughout all our talks, your mother insisted that she was acting under no kind of pressure, that she had no complaint against either of you at all, that you both did your very best to live amicably with her, and in fact, that the only thing that caused her any hesitation at all over surrendering her house was the fear that you or others might feel that she was hurt or offended."

Dr. Fisher coughed, bent down, produced a familiar volume from under the counter and laid it before them.

"So strongly and sincerely did your mother insist on this point that a bell rang loudly in my mind. I suddenly realized exactly what she was doing. As a Hertham householder, she was making what is technically called an 'act of total voluntary dispossession.' Checking up in my Peterstone and Rockcliff here, I established that by making this decision, she had unwittingly qualified herself for a very special award under the Godfrey Bequest—a most coveted award too. I was able to break the good news to her this morning shortly before you came in. The Book of Common Law leaves us in no doubt about her position. By the terms of this particular clause in the will, which comes under article thirty-one, she short-circuits any further collecting of references. She goes straight onto the Waiting List. More than that, she is immediately awarded a record card with full points, formally signed and sealed by Sir Alph Godfrey, Christopher, and the company secretary."

"You mean she now goes straight forward for interview before the Allocation Committee?" Bernard asked. "Just like that?"

"In her case the interview will be a pure formality. The

fully made-up record card, formally sealed in the company's name, is of course a direct passport to a house. There can be no question now. That's what makes this award one of the rarest and most valuable. It's a direct grant under what we call the IHS provision—that is the Immediate Home Selection provision."

"Couldn't we too . . . ," Marie began, then shook her head. "No, of course not."

"Your mother was totally ignorant of what she stood to gain."

"Yes," Marie said quietly, "but she did call the helpline."

"She called the helpline," Dr. Fisher reiterated rather solemnly. "And by doing so, she automatically gained honorary membership in the Society of Waiters."

Bernard felt strangely limp. None of the possible emotions, possible reactions, to sudden news, good or bad, seemed appropriate.

"You will have to congratulate her on her acquisition of a home just when you will be receiving congratulations your-selves on the progress you have made. There will be a mutual interchange of congratulations. It will be the occasion for some kind of celebration."

Bernard's limpness became faintness. Was it the heat of the office? Or was it the confusion of unarticulated emotional pres-sures mysteriously calling for some outburst that incongruously accommodated ingredients of joy and sadness, appreciation and disappointment, contentment and self-pity? The room began to swim before his eyes.

"Aren't you feeling well, Bernard?" he heard Marie ask.

"We must open the window," the voice of Dr. Fisher said as from a remote distance.

Consciously back in his own bedroom on earth, Bernard was awake some time before he could gather his thoughts together clearly enough to be able to trust himself to utterance.

"I had a funny dream," he said, understating the case. "Very interesting, really."

"Interesting!" the nurse said. "I like that! You were enjoying yourself. And here were we, just waiting . . . waiting . . ."

Harry Blamires [pronounced so as to rhyme with "the fires"] once sat amid the pipe smoke of his Oxford professor, and later friend, C. S. Lewis, who guided him in his early work as a writer. He recalls private tutorials ("there was always a lot of laughing in his company") during which Lewis sat on his chesterfield, a tin of tobacco at one side and a packet of cigarettes at the other, helping himself to these alternately. He was with Lewis one evening about the time the Narnia books were coming out, and they talked about the illustrations. Lewis was excited by a particular picture of Aslan. He dived down to a bottom shelf of a bookcase, picked up a volume, opened it, and laid it on Harry's knees—a French edition of *The Lion, the Witch and the Wardrobe*. "That's what I mean," Lewis said, pointing to a picture of Aslan leaping, streaking across the page, massive and powerful, almost terrifying. Harry recalls, "All the cuddliness was gone. There could be no question of stroking this awesome beast."

Today Harry continues the masterful storytelling he learned from his home in Keswick, in the scenic countryside of Cumbria, England's most northwestern country, known for its beautiful mountains and lakes.

He is known for thirteen theological and seventeen English literature books published in the United Kingdom and the United States, including *The Christian Mind* and *The Post-Christian Mind*—both referenced from pulpits and in theological discussion today. Several of his theological books, including those two, are currently being reissued by Regent College Publishing, Vancouver, British Columbia. His literary commentary on

Ulysses (*The New Bloomsday Book: A Guide through Ulysses*) is a celebrated classic, considered the quintessential guide to James Joyce's masterpiece.

To devote time to writing, Harry took an early retirement in 1976 from his post as head of the English department and then dean of arts and sciences at King Alfred's College, Winchester. He was awarded a doctorate in literature degree from the University of Southampton in 1993 for his work as a writer. He lectured widely in the United States in the 1970s and 1980s, notably as a visiting professor of English literature at Wheaton College in 1987.

Harry is married to Nancy Blamires, author of *Looking on Glass: Thoughts for Every Day*, a collection of meditations. They have five sons, all happily married.

For more on the writing process for *New Town*, its symbolism, and book group discussion questions, visit the Baker Publishing Group website (www.BakerPublishingGroup.com) and key in the book title.